P9-CDB-404

I squatted behind the "plate." Flip stood a few feet behind me with the radar gun and pointed it toward Satch.

This was the moment. We weren't just going to witness history, we were going to *make* history.

I was a little nervous. I'm pretty good with the glove, but I had never caught anyone who threw really hard. Satch himself said that Josh Gibson wouldn't be able to hit what he couldn't see. What if I couldn't see the ball coming at me? I made sure the catcher's mask was strapped on tight.

"I'll start you off nice and slow and easy," Satch said.

I put the mitt up and got ready to receive the pitch. I watched his motion carefully so I'd see the ball the whole way. He brought his arms high over his head really slowly, kicked up his leg, and—

Also by Dan Gutman

The Get Rich Quick Club

Johnny Hangtime

My Weird School:

Mr. Hynde is Out of His Mind!

Mrs. Cooney Is Loony!

Ms. LaGrange Is Strange!

Miss Lazar Is Bizarre!

Mr. Docker Is off His Rocker!

Baseball Card Adventures:

Honus & Me

Jackie & Me

Babe & Me

Shoeless Joe & Me

Mickey & Me

Abner & Me

Satch & Me

A Baseball Card Adventure

Dan Gutman

 HarperTrophy®
An Imprint of HarperCollins*Publishers*

Amistad

Harper Trophy® is a registered trademark of
HarperCollins Publishers.

Amistad is an imprint of HarperCollins Publishers.

Satch & Me
Copyright © 2006 by Dan Gutman
All rights reserved. Printed in the United States of America. No part of this book may be used or
reproduced in any manner whatsoever without written permission except in the case of brief
quotations embodied in critical articles and reviews. For information address HarperCollins Children's
Books, a division of HarperCollins Publishers, 10 East 53rd Street, New York, NY 10022.
www.harpercollinschildrens.com

Library of Congress Cataloging-in-Publication Data
Gutman, Dan.
  Satch & me : a baseball card adventure / Dan Gutman.—1st ed.
    p. cm.
  Summary: With his ability to travel through time using vintage baseball cards, Joe takes Flip with
him to find out whether Satchel Paige really was the fastest pitcher ever.
  ISBN 978-0-06-059493-0
  1. Paige, Satchel, 1906-1982—Juvenile fiction. [1. Paige, Satchel, 1906-1982—Fiction. 2. Baseball—
Fiction. 3. Time travel—Fiction. 4. Negro Leagues—Fiction. 5. African Americans—Fiction.
6. Segregation—Fiction.] I. Title: Satch and me. II. Title.
PZ7.G9846Sat 2006   2005005717
[Fic]—dc22   CIP
                                                                               AC

12 13 14   LP/BR   10 9 8 7 6 5 4
❖
First Harper Trophy edition, 2009

To all the great kids, librarians, and
teachers at the schools I visited in 2005

Acknowledgments

Thanks to Bill Burdick of the National Baseball Hall of Fame; John Zajc, Wayne Stivers, and Larry Lester of the Society for American Baseball Research; Marilyn Holt of the Carnegie Library of Pittsburgh; John Holway; my wife, Nina Wallace; and all the folks at HarperCollins Children's Books.

Many thanks also to the great people I met at the schools I visited in 2005:

In Alabama: Brookwood, Mountain Brook, and Cherokee Bend schools in Mountain Brook.

In Arizona: Desert Sun, Pima, Desert Canyon, Laguna, Hohokam, Cochise, Sonoran Sky, and ANLC schools in Scottsdale.

In Connecticut: Ledyard Center School in Ledyard; Butler School in Mystic; Noank School in Noank; Fairfield Country Day School in Fairfield; and Adams, Cox, Jones, Guilford Lakes, and Baldwin Middle School in Guilford.

In Georgia: Lovett School in Atlanta and Dolvin

School in Alpharetta.

In Iowa: Welton and Ekstrand Schools in Welton, Briggs School in Maquoketa, and Camanche School in Camanche.

In Massachusetts: Fessenden School in West Newton and Tenacre County Day School and Fiske School in Wellesley.

In Michigan: Forest, Longacre, Flanders, Gill, Hillside, Beechview, Wooddale, Wood Creek, Eagle, HCC, Lanigan, Grace, and Kenbrook Schools in Farmington Hills.

In Minnesota: Groveland School in Minnetonka, Deephaven School in Wayzata, and Minnewashta School in Excelsior.

In New Jersey: Horace Mann School in Cherry Hill, Strawbridge School in Haddon Township, Tatem and Lizzie Haddon Schools in Haddonfield, Yellin School in Stratford, Indian Fields School in Dayton, Deerfield School in Short Hills, Roosevelt School in River Edge, Stillwater School in Stillwater, McGinn School in Scotch Plains, Lincoln School in Nutley, H. B. Whitehorne Middle School and Brown School in Verona, Chatham Middle School in Chatham, Deerfield School in Mountainside, Yardville School in Yardville, and Hartford School in Mount Laurel.

In New York: Mount Kisco School in Mount Kisco, Bronxville School in Bronxville, Jefferson School in New Rochelle, and Riverdale Country School in the Bronx.

In Oklahoma: Washington, Eisenhower, Madison, Truman, Wilson, Jackson, Cleveland, Roosevelt, Kennedy, and Monroe Schools in Norman.

In Oregon: Errol Hassell School in Aloha; Scholls Heights and Cooper Mountain Schools in Beaverton; and Wismer, Ridgewood, West Tualatin View, and Montclair Schools in Portland.

In Pennsylvania: Colonial School in Plymouth Meeting; Friends Central School in Wynnewood; Seville, Perrysville, and Ross Schools in Pittsburgh; Jenkintown School in Jenkintown; Newtown Friends School in Newtown; Annville School in Annville; Paradise and Salisbury Schools in Pequea Valley; Buckingham School in Buckingham; and Cold Spring, Gayman, and Kutz Schools in Doylestown.

In Rhode Island: Dunn's Corners School in Westerly and Bradford School in Bradford.

So, who is the fastest pitcher in baseball?
Nobody really knows.

— *Baseball Almanac, 2003*

1

Run on Anything

"THIS GUY AIN'T SO FAST, STOSH," MY COACH, FLIP Valentini, hollered. "He can't pitch his way out of a paper bag."

We were at Dunn Field playing the Exterminators, probably the weirdest team in the Louisville Little League. Most of the teams in our league are sponsored by doctors, hardware stores, or banks. *Normal* businesses, you know? But these guys are sponsored by an *exterminator*. Whoever heard of a Little League team sponsored by a company that kills bugs?

On the front of their uniforms, the Exterminators have their logo (a squashed ant) and on the back they have their phone number (1-800-GOT-BUGS). It looks really stupid. They even have their own cheer, which they insist on rapping along with a drum machine before they take the field. It goes like this . . .

Stomp 'em! Spray 'em!
That's the way we play 'em!
We send the pests back to their nests!
When we turn the lights on,
It's lights out for YOUUUUUUUU!

Man, I'd be embarrassed if I had to play on that team.

The Exterminators even have a mascot. Before each game, some little kid dressed up like a roach runs out on the field. They call him Buggy. The whole team chases Buggy around the infield. When they catch him, they pretend to beat the crap out of him. Or at least it *looks* like they're pretending. The mascot is probably the little brother of one of the kids on the team.

It's all very entertaining, and the moms and dads in the bleachers get a big kick out of it. I must admit, even I get a kick out of it.

The thing about the Exterminators, though, is that these guys can flat out *play*. Usually when a team has a dumb gimmick, that's *all* they have. They can't hit, can't pitch, can't run, and they can't field. They put on a show because they're no good. But the Exterminators won the Louisville Little League championship last season, and they really know the fundamentals of baseball. They always throw to the right base. They always hit the cutoff man. Their coach must know what he's talking about.

But we're pretty good too. Our team, Flip's Fan

Club, is sponsored by a local baseball card shop that's owned by our coach, Flip Valentini. Sponsors don't usually get involved with the team, other than paying for the uniforms and bats and stuff. But to Flip, owning our team is like owning the Yankees. He lives and breathes for us. He's our owner, manager, third base coach, and even our chauffeur if our moms are late or their cars break down.

Our team doesn't do any silly rap songs. But we can play solid baseball, because Flip taught us everything he knows. And believe me, Flip Valentini has forgotten more about baseball than most people ever learn.

Our problem is that the Exterminators have this one kid named Kyle who we nicknamed Mutant Man. Kyle must be some kind of genetic freak. He's only thirteen, like most of us, but he's six feet tall and he's got these long arms. Mutant arms. His arms are so long, it's like he's a different species or something.

Mutant Man doesn't bother with a curveball. He doesn't have a changeup or any other kind of trick pitches. All he's got is his fastball. But he just lets loose and *brings it* with every pitch. He's a lefty, and when Kyle lets go of the ball, watch out. With those arms, you feel like he's releasing the ball right in front of your face.

It's especially hard for a left-handed batter like me, because the pitch seems like it's coming at you from the first base dugout. *Scary*. It's almost impossible to stay in the batter's box because the ball looks like it's going to take your head off. Then, while you're bailing out, it shoots across the plate, and the next thing you know the ump is yelling, "Strike three!"

One dominating pitcher can take a team a long way. Kyle the Mutant Man has struck me out a whole bunch of times. He's struck us *all* out a bunch of times. In fact, we've never beaten the guy. Once, he struck out fifteen of us in six innings. That's just about *impossible*.

But this time, we had Mutant Man in trouble. It was the bottom of the sixth inning, which is the last inning in our league. The Mutant was shutting us out as usual, but our pitcher, Jason Shounick, had pitched a pretty good game too. He had given up only two runs.

Blake Butler grounded out to second base to start the inning. Tanner Havens fouled off a bunch of pitches, and he finally worked out a walk. I was up, and I represented the tying run.

In case you're not a big baseball fan, when you "represent the tying run," it means that if you can find a way to score, the game will be tied. A homer would be the quickest, simplest way to do it.

But I wasn't even thinking about hitting a homer. No way I was going to take Kyle the Mutant over the wall. I just wanted to get the bat on the ball. If I could push it past one of the infielders and get on base, one of our other guys might be able to drive me and Tanner in. That's all I hoped for. Make something happen. Just make contact.

As I stepped into the batter's box, I was giving myself advice. "Don't bail out," I said. "Don't bail out. Even if it looks like it's going to hit you, stay in there."

I decided not to swing at the first pitch no matter how good it looked. If I could just stay in the batter's box without stepping backward, it would be a small victory.

Mutant Man looked in for a sign, even though everybody on the field knew he only had one pitch. I tried to relax my grip on the bat.

"You can do it, Stosh!" Ryan Younghans shouted from our bench.

"He's a whiffer, Kyle!" somebody called from the bleachers.

The Mutant glared at me, and I glared right back. Then he went into that big windup. I stood there and let the ball go by. Tanner took off from first. The catcher jumped up and whipped the ball to second. Tanner slid in and the ump called him safe.

It was strike one on me, but now we had a guy at second. A single could score him and make it 2-1.

Mutant Man turned around and looked at the base runner. I took a deep breath and closed my eyes for a moment. Maybe Mutant Man was a little nervous now. He wasn't used to worrying about base runners. I decided to swing if the next pitch looked hittable.

I don't even know if I ever saw the pitch, to tell you the truth. I just tried to get my bat out there the way Flip taught us. Somehow, I got lucky and hit something. It wasn't pretty, but the ball went dribbling down the first base line.

Hey, I didn't care. I was digging for first. The first baseman dove to his left, but the ball snuck between his glove and the first base bag. It was fair by inches.

The ball skipped down the right field line and suddenly everybody was yelling. People were yelling for me to run (like I didn't know that!). People were yelling for Tanner to score. People were yelling for the right fielder to get the ball. People were yelling for the third baseman to get ready for the throw.

That's where I was heading. No way I was going to stop at second. I knew the right fielder was the worst kid on their team and he probably wouldn't be able to throw me out at third. I didn't even look up for a sign from Flip, who was coaching over there. I slid in and kicked up a spray of dirt, partly to make it hard for the third baseman to tag me and partly, I must admit, because kicking up a spray of dirt is fun and looks way cool.

I got up and dusted myself off while everybody went crazy. Tanner had scored. I was on third. Flip clapped me on the back. The guys on the Exterminators were looking anxious for the first time all day. We had finally scored a run, and I was on third with a good chance of scoring another one.

Exterminators	0	1	0	1	0	0
Flip's Fan Club	0	0	0	0	0	1

We were only down by one run.

I scanned the bleachers to see if I could find my mom anywhere. It was pretty easy. She was behind first base, jumping up and down and screaming. "Did you see my Joey? Did you see that hit?"

I wished she would calm down a little. It's embarrassing, and it's not cool. When she's jumping up and down and going crazy, it looks like I must totally suck most of the time and I got lucky for a change. If she would be calm after I hit a triple, it would look like I'm a good player and she *expected* me to hit a triple. As it was, it was a dinky little hit. Nothing to write home about.

Besides, it wouldn't mean a thing if we lost the game. I turned my attention back to the field. Flip leaned over to me and whispered in my ear.

"Run on anything, Stosh. On the crack of the bat, burn rubber."

Flip grew up in Brooklyn, New York, and he talks sort of like those guys you see in old black-and-white movies.

"You sure, Flip?" I asked.

"Never been more sure."

I didn't get it. There was one out. Baseball wisdom says that you run on anything when there are *two* outs. Everybody knows that.

Running on anything with two outs makes sense, because if the batter makes an out, it's three outs and the side is retired. But if the batter gets a hit and you were off with the crack of the bat, you get a big jump toward the next base, or home plate in my case.

The reason why you don't run on anything when there are *less* than two outs is because if the batter makes an out, your team will still have one or two chances to drive you in. So you don't want to risk getting tagged out and kill a rally.

If that didn't make any sense to you, don't worry about it. It doesn't matter. Baseball is a complicated game. But that's why I like it. The point is, Flip ordered me to run on anything with one out.

Maybe Flip knew something I didn't know, I figured. The guy is really old, somewhere in his seventies. Wisdom comes with age, isn't that what they say? Maybe Flip spotted something I didn't see. Maybe that's why he told me to run on anything even though there was only one out.

Anyway, I'm not the kind of guy who questions his coach's judgment. If Flip tells me to run on anything, I run.

"Whatever you say, Flip."

Mike Baugh, our second baseman, was up. He likes to swing at the first pitch. I took a short lead off third. The last thing I wanted was to get picked off by Mutant Man. He looked over at me, then at

Mike. He let the ball fly, and as expected, Mike took a rip at it.

"Go!" Flip ordered me when we heard the crack of the bat.

When I say "the crack of the bat," I don't just mean the sound of the bat hitting the ball. Mike's bat actually cracked! It broke in half!

Now, I've seen wooden bats break plenty of times. But Mike was swinging a metal bat. The thing broke in two, and the fat part was flying right at me. I didn't even see where the ball went. I ducked under the flying bat head and tore home.

The catcher didn't look like he was ready for a play at the plate. But I didn't trust him. He might be trying to deke me. I slid into home headfirst, which looks really cool. Tie game.

But almost immediately, I sensed something was wrong.

"Go back!" everybody on our bench was screaming at me. "It's a pop-up! Get *back*!"

I jumped up and dashed back toward third. Out of the corner of my eye I could see the shortstop backpedaling onto the outfield grass. I was running as fast as I could. The shortstop caught the pop-up and whipped the ball to third base. I slid in, but the third baseman stuck his glove with the ball in it between my foot and the third base bag.

"You're out!" hollered the ump. "That's the ball game, boys."

I was exhausted. I lay there in the dirt. Everybody

started yelling at me.

"You bonehead!" Jason yelled. "You cost us the game, Stosh!"

"What are you, a moron?" yelled Tanner. "There was only one out!"

The kids on the Exterminators were laughing their heads off. "Nice slide, Stoshack," one of them yelled. "Maybe you oughta learn how to count!"

I looked up at Flip. He was counting on his fingers, looking more confused than ever.

2

The Radar Gun

NUMBERS AND STATISTICS ARE PRETTY IMPORTANT IN baseball. Strikes. Balls. Outs. The score. Batting order. Innings. You've got to remember a lot of numbers. And if you forget a number as simple as how many outs there are in a crucial situation, you could be in big trouble.

I was in big trouble.

"There was *one out*, Stoshack!" hollered Blake. "You don't run on anything with one out!"

"You are such an idiot!" Mike said. "This one's gonna go down in history, man."

I wasn't going to tell them that Flip messed up by ordering me to run on anything and costing us the game. Ever since my parents split up and my dad got hurt in a car crash, Flip has been like a father to me. I'd rather take the heat for not knowing how many outs there were than make Flip look bad. It was an honest mistake. I just hung my head and went to pack up my stuff.

I was putting my glove in my duffel bag when Flip shuffled over to our dugout.

"Gather 'round, guys," he said. "Listen up."

Everybody stopped putting away their gear.

"Stosh wasn't the one who screwed up," he said. "It was my fault. I told him to run on anything. I thought there were two outs. I'm the bonehead. I'm sorry."

It was real quiet. You don't hear grown-ups apologizing to kids very often, even when they're wrong. It may have been a first.

"Maybe I'm gettin' too old for this," Flip said, sitting down heavily on the bench.

I've had a few coaches in my years of playing ball, but none of them took winning and losing as seriously as Flip. To him, every game was like the seventh game of the World Series. We win some and we lose some, but this was the first time one of Flip's decisions lost the game for us. He looked so sad. I thought he might cry or something.

"It's just a game, Flip," I told him.

"Yeah, fuhgetaboutit, Mr. Valentini," said Jason.

"We'll get 'em next time, Coach," Blake said.

I guess the other guys felt sorry for Flip too. Everybody was telling him all the stuff our coaches have always told us over the years when we did something dumb and blew a game.

"Y'know, I used to be young and sharp," Flip said.

"My mind was like a steel trap. Now I can't remember where I put my glasses some days. Can't remember where I put my car keys in the mornin'. . . ."

"It's okay, Mr. Valentini," Tanner assured him. "You're still the best coach, man."

"I used to pitch, y'know," Flip continued. He closed his eyes, like he was remembering something from long ago. "I could really bring some heat in my day. Almost had a tryout with the Dodgers."

"Really?" we all said. I knew he rooted for "Dem Bums" as he always called them. But he never told me he was good enough to play for them.

"Big-league teams used to hold open tryouts back when I was young," Flip said. "Guys could walk in off the street and give it their best shot. I saw a notice in *The Brooklyn Daily Eagle*. It said to go to Ebbets Field that Saturday if you wanted to try out. But I didn't go."

"Why not, Flip?" I asked.

"My mother said I had to do chores."

"Chores!?" everybody yelled.

"Sounds like my mom," Mike said.

"You mean you could've had the chance to play for the Dodgers, but you had to do *chores* instead?" asked Jason. None of us could believe it.

"That's child abuse, Mr. Valentini," said Blake. "You should've sued your mother."

"Oh, I don't know that I woulda made the Dodgers," Flip said. "Prob'ly not. My control wasn't too good. But I could throw the ball *hard*. Guys were afraid to hit against me. I always wished I'd tried out. I coulda done my chores later. I coulda . . ."

Flip's voice trailed off. Nobody said a word. I couldn't think of anything that would cheer him up.

Looking at Flip, it's hard to imagine that he was young once. He's a little stooped over, his hair is white, and the skin hangs off his neck and arms all loose, like it's one size too big for his bones.

I don't know too much about Flip's personal life. He's got a sister, but she lives in Texas and they don't see each other much. He doesn't have any kids, and he never got married. We're like the only family he has. His life is coaching our team and managing the store.

I always felt bad that he went home at the end of the day to a crummy apartment all by himself. There aren't a lot of old ladies around Louisville, as far as I know. One time Tanner said he could fix Flip up with his grandmother, who lives just across the Ohio River in Sellersburg, Indiana. We all laughed, and Flip said he wasn't interested. There used to be this little old lady named Amanda Young who lived next door to me. But she sort of disappeared. It's a long story.

"Hey, put that junk away," Flip said suddenly. We all looked over at Mike, who had a bag of Doritos in his hand. "Don't be putting that crap in your body, Mikey. You wanna be needin' a triple bypass when you're fifty?"

After he had a heart attack years back, Flip

turned into a real health nut. The only thing he lets us eat in the dugout is sunflower seeds. The tasteless, unsalted kind.

"There's somethin' I wanna show you fellas," Flip said, reaching into an equipment bag. "Almost forgot this too. I'd forget my head if it wasn't attached to my shoulders."

He pulled out this machine that looked sort of like a handheld hair dryer, but there was no cord to plug in.

"What's that, Flip, a ray gun?" asked Jason.

"Yeah, next time we lose, Flip's gonna zap us," said Blake, and everybody laughed.

"No, you bums," Flip said. "Ain't you never seen a radar gun before?"

I had. They clock the speed of a pitch. Somebody sits behind home plate and points the gun at the pitcher. The gun registers the speed of the pitch in miles per hour. Usually when you watch a game on TV, they show the velocity of each pitch. That's because somebody is clocking it with a radar gun.

"Those things are cool," said Tanner.

"See," Flip explained, "the gun shoots out a microwave beam—"

"Can that thing make popcorn?" asked Blake, and a few guys laughed.

"Very funny, Blake. The microwave bounces off the movin' baseball and then it goes back in here," Flip continued. "The gun calculates the difference in frequency between the original wave and

the reflected wave, and then it translates that information into miles per hour."

"Can we try it, Flip?" asked Jason, who can probably throw harder than anyone on our team.

"Well, whaddaya think I brung it for?" Flip said.

Flip had us line up in alphabetical order at the
pitcher's mound. He told Ryan to put on the catcher's gear and get behind the plate. Flip stood behind
him with the gun and pointed it at the pitcher's
mound. He fiddled with the buttons.

Flip said we could each throw five pitches. Rob
Anderson, who couldn't pitch if his life depended on
it, got to throw first.

"Now, I don't want you bums hurtin' yourselves,"
Flip told us. "Throw the first two nice and easy. Just
lob 'em in. Put a little more on your third and fourth
pitch. And on your last throw, give it all you got."

"What does that thing go up to?" asked Rob.

"Don't worry, Anderson," said Flip. "You ain't
gonna break it."

Rob gripped the ball and went into a really pathetic
windup. The ball went sailing over Ryan, over Flip,
and over the backstop. Everybody cracked up.

"Try again," Flip said. "That one didn't register.
Nice and easy, now."

Rob threw one reasonably near the plate. Flip
looked at the back of the gun.

"Twenty-two miles per hour," he announced. We
just about fell all over ourselves laughing. Everybody
knows that a major league fastball is around 90 miles

per hour, and a few pitchers can even crack 100.

"I could *walk* the ball to the plate faster than that," cracked Blake.

"Knock it off, Blake," Flip said. "You ain't no Sandy Koufax either."

Rob got a little better with his next three pitches, but the best he could do was 36 miles per hour. I knew I could throw harder than *that*. Some of the guys were snickering. But I wasn't. There was always the chance that I'd make a fool of myself too.

Mike Baugh was next. He pitches for us sometimes, and he's got a decent arm. In four pitches, the gun recorded 35, 38, 43, and 50 miles per hour.

"Okay, cut it loose now, Mikey," said Flip.

Mike reared back and gave it everything he had.

"Fifty-nine miles per hour!" Flip shouted.

I was surprised. It looked like Mike was throwing pretty fast, but major league pitchers can throw 40 miles per hour *faster*. It was hard to believe.

We went through the line one at a time. Most of the guys reached the 50s on their final pitch, and one or two guys reached the 60s. Jason clocked 67 miles per hour on one pitch.

I'd like to say that when it was my turn I threw the ball so hard that the gun registered "Wow!" or "Sign the kid up!" But the truth is, my hardest pitch was only 56 miles per hour. Pretty weak.

After we all had a turn, the guys started getting on their bikes or drifting over to the parking lot, where some of the parents were waiting in their cars.

"How fast could *you* throw, Flip?" asked Tanner. "I mean, in your prime."

"Geez, I dunno," Flip said. "They didn't have these gizmos when I was in my prime."

"Hey, Flip," I asked, "how fast was the fastest fastball?"

Flip scratched his head.

"Well, guys like Roger Clemens, Randy Johnson, and Nolan Ryan clocked 100 miles an hour," Flip told us. "A few other guys too. Maybe 102, 103 even."

"No, I mean *ever*."

"You wanna know who threw the fastest pitch *ever*?"

"Yeah," I said.

"Well, they've only had radar guns since the 1970s," Flip said. "Guys like Walter Johnson and Bobby Feller and Satchel Paige were plenty fast in their day. But they all pitched long before the 70s. There was no way to clock 'em."

"Couldn't they take old movies of those guys and figure out how fast they threw?" asked Jason.

"Guys like Cy Young were pitching even before they had movie cameras," Flip said. "Nobody knows how fast those guys threw the ball. It's one of those mysteries that'll never be solved, I guess."

I looked at the radar gun. Then I looked at Flip. Flip looked at me. Then he looked at the radar gun.

I wondered if Flip was thinking what I was thinking.

3

The Fastest Fastball

THERE'S SOMETHING YOU NEED TO UNDERSTAND ABOUT me. I've got a secret power.

No, I can't read minds. I can't fly and I can't predict the future and I can't communicate with the dead or anything weird like that. My secret power is that I can travel through time. Not only that, but I can travel through time with baseball cards.

Oh, go ahead and yuk it up. Have your little laugh. I don't care. Whether you believe me or not, I've had this power for a long time. When I pick up certain baseball cards, I get this weird tingling sensation in my fingertips. Have you ever touched a TV screen really lightly, and felt that static electricity on your fingers? That's what it feels like when I touch certain baseball cards.

If I drop the card right away, nothing happens. But if I keep holding it, the tingling sensation

19

gradually moves up my arm, across my body, and down my legs. In about five seconds, I completely disappear from this world and appear back in the past.

If I'm holding a 1919 baseball card, it will take me to the year 1919. If I'm holding a 1932 card, I'll show up in 1932. It's just about the coolest thing in the world. As far as I know, nobody else can do it. But I *can* take people with me when I go back in time. I know that because I've done it.

The power seems to have become stronger. Or maybe I'm just getting better at it with practice. Under the right conditions, I can even send myself back through time with a plain old photograph. But baseball cards work best, and especially older cards.

I don't exactly go around bragging about my "special gift." That's what my mom calls it. A special gift. I don't want the kids at school thinking I'm some kind of a freak. The only people who know about it are my mom and dad, my uncle Wilbur, who's really old, and my annoying cousin Samantha. Oh, and this really jerky kid named Bobby Fuller who has always hated me. But he doesn't even play in our league anymore. He's into football now.

There's just one other person who knows I can travel through time with baseball cards. Flip.

Flip didn't believe me at first. When I told him that I could travel through time with a baseball card, he just laughed in my face. So I went back to 1919 with an old card and brought back two pieces of paper signed by Shoeless Joe Jackson. His autograph was one of the most valuable in history. I gave them to Flip, and the money he got from selling those autographs saved his store from going out of business. Flip never doubted me again.

As soon as I got home from the game against the Exterminators, I called up Flip.

"Are you thinking what I'm thinking?" I asked.

"Well, that depends on what you're thinkin', Stosh."

"I'm thinking that I could take a radar gun back in time with me," I said. "I could take it back to the time before they had radar guns, and I could track the speed of pitches. It would be cool to find out who was the fastest pitcher in baseball history."

"That's exactly what I was thinkin'," Flip said. "Great minds think alike."

Flip got all excited. He's a member of this organization called SABR. It stands for Society for American Baseball Research. They're a bunch of die-hard baseball fans who devote themselves to digging up facts and stats that nobody knows about. Like, one guy might devote his life to counting how many times Lou Gehrig got a hit on a 3-1 count when he was playing away games in July. Stuff like that. Some of them are obsessed, if you ask me.

Anyway, Flip is really into baseball history, and the idea of finding out who was the fastest pitcher appealed to him.

"One problem, though," he said.

"What?"

"I borrowed the radar gun from the coach of the

high school baseball team. I promised him I'd give it back to him as soon as I'm done with it."

"Can't I just borrow it for a day or two?" I asked. "He'll never know I had it."

"These guns cost a bundle," Flip told me. "If something happened to it, the coach would go nuts. He'd have my head."

"Oh, come on, Flip!" I begged. "Nothing's gonna happen. I promise. I'll be real careful with it."

He was quiet for a few seconds, and I thought he was about to cave, but he didn't.

"I'm sorry, Stosh," Flip finally said. "These guns are delicate. I'm responsible for it. I gotta make sure I return it to the high school in perfect condition."

That's when I got a brainstorm.

"What if you went *with* me, Flip?" I asked.

"Went with you where?"

"Back in time!" I said. "We'll go back and meet guys like Walter Johnson and Bob Feller and the others. We'll see how fast they *really* were. We'll find out who was the fastest pitcher in baseball history! Can you imagine? When we get back and you tell everybody what you found, you'll be like the king of SABR, Flip!"

"Oh, they'd never believe me."

"I won't touch the gun," I begged. "You can hold it the whole time. Oh, come on, Flip. If nothing else, it'll be fun!"

Again, I thought I had him. There was silence at

the other end of the line. He was thinking it over.

"Stosh, I'm seventy-two years old," he said wearily. "I don't fly no more. With my crappy vision, I shouldn't even be drivin' my car. I can't be doin' somethin' crazy like travelin' through time."

"Please?"

"Adventure is for the young," Flip said. "I've had enough excitement for my life."

"Oh man, Flip!" I said. "You never go anywhere. Just think of it. We'll get to meet those old-time players you're always talking about. We can tell Cy Young they named an award after him. It will be so cool!"

"I'm sorry, Stosh. No can do."

Well, that was that. I gave it my best shot. Baseball historians would just have to keep on speculating which pitcher was the fastest. I hung up with Flip and went upstairs to take off my uniform. Then I got started on my homework.

Later that night, I was playing a computer game when the phone rang. My mom picked it up and hollered that Flip was calling for me.

"I thought it over," Flip said. "I'm in."

4

Our Guy

FLIP'S FAN CLUB IS A LITTLE STORE IN A STRIP MALL OFF Shelbyville Road on the east side of Louisville. It's only about a mile from my house, so I usually bike over.

When I went to see Flip the next day, I locked my bike to a No Skateboarding sign outside. The little bell jangled when I pulled the door open. There weren't any customers inside. Flip was behind the counter reading an old *Invincible Iron Man* comic book.

Flip doesn't just sell baseball cards. He sells comics, Star Wars action figures, those old-time metal lunch boxes, and all kinds of collectibles from a long time ago. On one wall Flip has a bunch of black-and-white photos of the old Brooklyn Dodgers—Jackie Robinson, Pee Wee Reese, Duke Snider. You never know what you're going to find in Flip's Fan Club.

"Stosh!" Flip looked up when I came in. "I been waitin' ferya!"

Flip pulled some big books out from behind the counter. There were yellow Post-it notes sticking out of some of the pages.

"I did a little research," Flip said as he opened one of the books.

So did I. I have a copy of *The Baseball Encyclopedia* at home, which lists the complete statistics for every player who ever appeared in a major league game. It's more than two thousand pages long, and about four inches thick.

The only problem is that statistics don't always tell the whole story. There were some really great pitchers who won a lot of games even though they weren't known for overpowering speed. Guys like Tom Seaver and Greg Maddux won because of their control, location, and smarts. But all I wanted to know was who threw the fastest pitch in baseball history.

"Walter Johnson," Flip said, pointing his bony finger at a picture in one of his books. "Now *he* was a pitcher. The Big Train, they used to call 'im. Awesome speed. Tall fella. Big sidearm motion. Murder on righties. He retired in 1927 with 417 wins and 110 shutouts. One year he led the American League in wins, games, strikeouts, starts, complete games, innings pitched, and shutouts. Can you imagine that? And he pitched for the Washington Senators, who were just about the worst team in baseball!"

"How fast was he?" I asked.

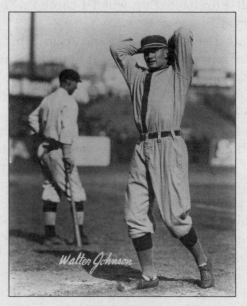

The Big Train

"Says here they clocked him at 99.7 miles per hour once," Flip said. "But that was in 1914, so it don't mean nothin'. They didn't have the technology to track speed accurately back then."

"It would be cool to go back in time and clock him with a radar gun," I said.

"We could do it," Flip said. "Wouldn't be hard to get a Johnson card."

The door jangled open and a little girl came in with her mother. They started looking at some girly stuff in the corner. Flip asked if they needed help, and the mom said they were just looking.

"Now, here's Bob Feller," Flip said, leaning toward me and lowering his voice a little. "Prob'ly the fastest guy in the late 1930s and 1940s. He fanned fifteen guys in his first big-league start, and he was still in high school! He claimed he was clocked at 107.9 miles per hour. That don't mean nothin' either. There's no proof."

"Do you have any Barbie cards?" the little girl suddenly asked.

"Sure," Flip replied. "I got a 1968 Velvet Suit Barbie and a 1969 Sailor Suit Barbie and I got three 1989 Dance Club Barbies. That's the one where she's wearin' a white leather jacket. Be-you-tiful. Mint condition too."

"We're looking for *new* Barbie cards," the girl's mom said. Flip wrinkled up his nose at the word "new" and rolled his eyes at me.

"But these come in a glitter plastic case," he added.

"No thanks." The girl and her mom left.

Flip pulled out one of his other books and opened to the pages he had marked with Post-it notes.

"There are so many old-time guys who threw hard," he said. "Back in the 1890s, Amos Rusie was so fast, they moved all the pitchers back just so hitters would have a chance against him. And Lefty Grove led the American League in strikeouts seven years running. They said he was so fast, he could throw a pork chop past a wolf."

"Look, here's Cy Young," Flip said. "Y'know he got his name because he was supposed to be as fast as a cyclone, right? He won 511 games. That's more than anybody else *ever*. Of course, he *lost* more games than anybody else too. 316 losses. Ouch!"

Cy Young

Flip really got into this baseball history stuff. Most of it was in his head. The books just refreshed his memory.

"Dizzy Dean, boy, he was fast," Flip continued, thumbing through pages. "Then there was this guy named Steve Dalkowski who was really fast and really wild. He never made it to the majors 'cause he couldn't get the ball over the plate. Then, of course, there was Satchel Paige."

I knew a little bit about Paige. My dad has a ball that was autographed by him. He told me that Paige pitched in the Negro Leagues back in the days when African American players weren't allowed to play in the majors. That was before Jackie Robinson broke the color barrier in 1947.

"We can't go visit *all* those guys, Flip," I said.

"You're right," he agreed. "We gotta pick one to be our guy."

Flip closed the books and turned on his computer, which was on the counter next to him. He went to Google and started searching for stuff.

"You know how to use the Internet, Flip?" I asked, a little surprised.

"What, ya think I drive a horse and buggy?" Flip said. "Howdya think I run this joint?"

Flip began to search for "fastest pitcher" and stuff like that. For an old guy, he knew his way around a mouse and keyboard pretty well.

"Listen to this quote," he said, reading off the screen. 'I know who's the best pitcher I ever seen and it's old Satchel Paige. My fastball looks like a change of pace alongside that little pistol bullet old Satchel shoots up to the plate.'"

"Who said that?" I asked.

"Dizzy Dean."

"Dean said Paige was faster than *he* was?" I asked.

"Yup."

"But if black players weren't allowed in the majors, how did Dizzy Dean know how fast Satchel Paige was?" I asked.

"In the off-season, they used to play exhibition games against each other," Flip told me. "In fact, Paige beat Dean in 1934. That's when Dizzy was at his peak. And Paige beat Feller too, in 1946."

"Twelve years later?" I asked.

"Paige pitched for somethin' like forty years," Flip said. "He was unbelievable. Hey, Stosh, check this out. Lefty Grove and Bob Feller *both* said Paige was the best pitcher they ever saw."

"Wow!" I had no idea Satchel Paige was so good. Flip kept finding more quotes about him.

"Ted Williams said Paige was the greatest pitcher in baseball," Flip said. "And Joe DiMaggio called him the fastest pitcher he ever faced."

"DiMaggio *and* Williams said Paige was the best pitcher ever?" I asked. "They were two of the best hitters ever!"

"Look, here's a quote from my man Dolf Camilli," Flip said. "He played first base for Brooklyn when I was growin' up. Camilli said, 'Satchel Paige threw me the fastest ball I've ever seen in my life.'"

Flip logged off, put his computer to sleep, and turned to me.

"Stosh, I think we found our guy."

Leroy "Satchel" Paige

5

The Auction

THE FIRST THING I DID WHEN I GOT HOME FROM FLIP'S
Fan Club was to look up Satchel Paige in *The
Baseball Encyclopedia*. It said he had a lifetime
major league record of 28 wins and 31 losses, plus
32 saves. Not very impressive. Of course, Paige
pitched for more than twenty years in the Negro
Leagues before they ever let him in the majors.

Flip called that night while I was doing my
homework. I figured he was calling to let me know
he was changing the time of practice, or something
like that. But no.

"I have bad news," he said. "We can't go back in
time to clock Satchel Paige's fastball."

"What?!" I said. "Why not?"

"I completely forgot," Flip said. "There are no baseball cards of Negro League players. They never made
any. I swear, I forget everything these days. Don't

grow old, Stosh. Memory is the first thing to go."

Flip told me that the only Negro League baseball cards are those "retro" cards that were printed in recent years, long after the league was gone. They wouldn't do me any good.

"Are you sure?" I asked.

"I called every card dealer I know," Flip said. "The only *real* Paige cards are from the 1950s, when he was pitching for St. Louis. But he was over the hill by then. It wouldn't be fair to clock his fastball when he was an old guy."

I was crushed, and Flip knew it. He kept apologizing for forgetting and he kept trying to come up with other solutions.

"What about Bob Feller?" Flip suggested. "I got a Feller card back at the store from 1946. That was the year he won 26 games and struck out 348 batters. Pitched ten shutouts that season too. Boy, he was fast."

"What would be the point?" I asked. "Even if we went back in time with the radar gun and clocked Feller, we'll never know how fast Paige was. Feller himself said that Paige was faster."

Flip apologized one more time, and then we hung up. That was that. I'd never find out who threw the fastest pitch in baseball history.

I pushed Satchel Paige out of my mind and went back to doing my homework. There was a big math test I had to study for, and I also had to look up some stuff on the Internet for social studies.

Well, I *tried* to push Satchel Paige out of my mind, anyway. Maybe Flip was wrong. Maybe there *was* a Paige card out there somewhere. Just for the heck of it, I typed in "www.ebay.com."

I don't know if you know about eBay or not. It's this online auction site where people who want to buy stuff and people who have stuff to sell can connect with each other. You can find all kinds of weird stuff on eBay. If anybody in the *world* had a Satchel Paige card to sell, I would find it there.

Here's how it works. Somebody who has something to sell lists the item, with a description of the thing and usually a photo. Buyers who want that item can place bids through their computers. There's a deadline for when the auction ends. When the deadline passes, whoever has the highest bid wins. You send the money to the seller and they send you the stuff that you bid on. It's pretty simple.

You have to be eighteen years old to buy or sell on eBay. But my dad said I could use his account. He buys stuff all the time. I bought a few baseball cards and some old magazines. I never sold anything.

The main eBay screen asks, "What are you looking for?" So I typed in "Satchel Paige."

A few seconds later, ten screens' worth of Satchel Paige items jumped to my computer screen. People were selling Satchel Paige autographs, jerseys, plaques, pencil clips, books, and collector plates with Satchel Paige's face on them. There were even Satchel Paige bobble-head dolls.

I had to narrow my search. I typed in "Satchel Paige card." If there were no Negro League baseball cards, the search would turn up nothing. That was what I expected.

But that's not what happened. There was one listing. It said: SATCHEL PAIGE PHOTO POSTCARD.

A postcard! I scrolled down to the description of the item. It said the postcard was from 1942 and it was in excellent condition.

Maybe I could use a postcard, I thought. After all, I had used a photograph to go back to 1863 and meet Abner Doubleday. A postcard with a photo on it might do the trick too.

The photo on the card was black and white. Satchel Paige was leaning way back and kicking his leg up high, ready to throw the ball.

Instinctively, I reached out and touched the image of Paige on the screen, as if that alone would send me back to 1942.

Nothing happened. No tingles or anything.

I looked at the information about the auction. There had been just two bids on the postcard in the last seven days. The starting bid was two dollars and the current bid was four dollars. It was cheap! The auction deadline was five hours away.

I checked out the seller, who was located in Spring Valley, California. You've got to be careful what you bid on, because some sellers will send you damaged stuff, or stuff that is nothing like the way they described it. Sometimes they'll just take your money and send you nothing.

But this seller had been selling stuff on eBay for a long time. He (or she) had a 99.5 percent positive feedback rating. I looked at the feedback reviews and they all said things like, "Great deal on neat item" . . . "Well wrapped, in good condition as promised" . . . "Fast shipment, highly recommend."

Maybe a photo postcard would work.

I decided to bid on the postcard. Even if it wouldn't send me back in time, I'd only have spent a few bucks. Plus, I'd have something cool to add to my card collection.

Now, I'm no dummy. I know how eBay works. If you make a bid, somebody will very often outbid you. So the trick is to wait until the auction is about to end, and *then* place your bid.

The auction was scheduled to end in five hours. I looked at the clock by my bed. It was 10:30 P.M. Five hours later would be 3:30 A.M. I set my alarm to wake me up at 3:15 A.M. I logged off eBay, brushed my teeth, said good night to my mom, and went to bed.

When the alarm started to beep in the middle of the night, I was groggy, but I remembered what I had to do. I went to the computer and quickly logged on to eBay. The Satchel Paige postcard was still at four dollars. Good. Nobody else had made a bid. There were fourteen minutes left in the auction. I typed in a bid for five dollars and sat back to wait for the YOU HAVE WON THIS AUCTION message.

A minute later, this message appeared on my screen:

YOU HAVE BEEN OUTBID BY ANOTHER BIDDER. (IF YOU'D LIKE, BID AGAIN.)

What?!

It said the current bid was now seven dollars. Somebody else out there was bidding on the same

37

item! There were twelve minutes left in the auction. I typed in a bid for ten dollars. That'll show 'em I'm serious, I thought to myself.

YOU HAVE BEEN OUTBID BY ANOTHER BIDDER . . . .

Oh, man! This creep was playing hardball! The current bid was up to twelve dollars. I checked my wallet. I had a twenty-dollar bill in there and some change. There were ten minutes left in the auction. I typed in a bid for fourteen dollars. No way the postcard was worth that much to anybody else. But I wanted it badly. A few more minutes ticked by.

YOU HAVE BEEN OUTBID. . . .

This was really pissing me off! It was just a stupid postcard. No one else needed it as badly as I did. The current bid was up to sixteen dollars. There were only six minutes left in the auction.

No way was I going to let this jerk get the postcard. I decided to treat it like a basketball game. I'd let the clock run down and go for a final shot just before the buzzer. If I made the highest bid just before time ran out, I'd be the winner.

There were five minutes left in the auction. I just sat there and stared at the screen.

Four.

Three.

Two.

With one minute left, I typed in my final bid. Twenty bucks. My allowance wasn't due for another two weeks. This was all the money I had. I waited as long as I could and then I hit the Enter key.

YOU HAVE BEEN OUTBID. . . .

In the words of the immortal Babe Ruth, "!@#$%&!!!"

What? How could I lose?! I was really bummed.

I turned off the computer and tried to go back to sleep. It wasn't easy. I kept thinking about the stupid auction. The only good thing that came out of it was that I still had my twenty bucks.

A few days later, there was a knock at the door. Flip Valentini was standing on the front porch.

"Hey, Stosh," he said, "guess what I just got?"

He pulled the Satchel Paige postcard out of his jacket pocket. It was in a plastic sleeve.

"Where'd you get *that*?" I asked.

"I bought it on eBay," he said gleefully. "Twenty-three bucks. Some bum kept tryin' to outbid me, but I beat 'im at the last second."

"That bum was *me*!" I yelled. "I was bidding for it!"

"You?" Flip said, laughing. "I coulda got it fer four stinkin' bucks if you hadn't been biddin' against me, you bum!"

"I didn't know it was *you*!" I said.

We were both laughing so hard it hurt.

Flip pulled the postcard out of its plastic sleeve and handed it to me. Just touching it made my fingertips tingle.

6

That Tingling Sensation

I WAS IN THE KITCHEN HAVING A SNACK THE NEXT DAY when the doorbell rang. Mom was upstairs, so I went to get it. I heard some strange guy outside, mumbling to himself in a weird voice.

"You dirty rat," he said, "you killed my brother."

Maybe I should call the police, I thought. This guy sounded like a nut. I peeked through the peephole in the front door to get a look at him.

It was Flip.

He was wearing a gray suit and a hat with a brim, so he looked like a gangster. He had one of those old-time hard-shell suitcases in one hand. His other hand kept jabbing the air while he repeated, "You dirty rat . . . you dirty rat . . ."

I opened the door.

Flip pointed a finger and poked me in the chest.

"You dirty rat, you killed my brother. It's gonna

be curtains for you, mister. Curtains!"

Except that he said "doity" for "dirty," and "brudder" for "brother," and "coytins" for "curtains."

"Flip, are you losing your mind?" I asked.

"Whatsa matter?" he said. "You don't like my Jimmy Cagney impersonation?"

"Jimmy who?"

"Cagney!" Flip said. "He was a great actor. Ain'tcha never seen *White Heat* or *Angels with Dirty Faces*? Ah, never mind. How do I look, Stosh? Do I look like a heavy?"

"A heavy what?" I asked.

"A heavy. That's what they used to call bad guys in the movies," Flip said. "Don't mess with me, sonny. I may be packing heat."

I had no idea what "heat" meant either, but I figured it must be something bad guys used to pack when they went on vacation.

"Nice suit, Flip," I said. "Did you go to one of those antique clothing stores?"

"Heck no," he replied, stepping through the doorway. "I went to my closet. I knew this suit would come back in style someday. Just goes to show you should never throw anything away. Still fits perfect, huh?"

Actually, the suit kind of hung off him. Flip must have been a lot more muscular when he was younger. I didn't want to hurt his feelings, though.

"You look great, Flip," I said. "Do you have the radar gun?"

"Right here."

Flip tapped his suitcase and put it down on the living-room table. It didn't open with a zipper. Instead, Flip clicked open two metal latches, one on each side.

"I brought some duds for you too."

He took out some old clothes that looked like a smaller version of what he was wearing. For all I knew, he had saved it since he was my age.

"Oh, man, I can't wear this stuff," I complained.

"Why not?" Flip said. "When you play ball, you wear a baseball uniform. When you go to church, you wear another uniform. And when you go to 1942, you gotta wear a different uniform. Come on. Put it on, or I'll murder ya."

Flip said "murder" like "moyda."

I went to the bathroom and put on the weird clothes. Looking at myself in the mirror, I actually thought I looked pretty cool. Flip said I looked like a young John Dillinger, whoever he was.

"Your mom knows we're doin' this, right, Stosh?" Flip asked.

"Of course."

"And she's okay with it?"

When I first discovered I had the power to travel through time with baseball cards, my mother wasn't exactly what you'd call supportive. She thought it was dangerous. She thought I might get hurt, or worse. She was right. I almost got killed a few times. But after I took her back to 1863 with me to

meet Abner Doubleday, she was hooked. I didn't
have to talk her into letting me go anymore.

"Believe me, Flip, she said it's okay. My mom is
totally into this."

At that, my mother came downstairs. Flip did one
of those wolf whistles guys do when they see a pretty
girl. I did a double take. Mom was wearing one of
those weird old dresses with shoulder pads, and her
hair was all pinned up on top of her head. Her lips and
fingernails were bright red. And she was singing. . . .

"'Don't sit under the apple tree with anyone
else but me," she sang, "anyone else but me, anyone else but me. . . .'"

Ugh. I can't believe old people think hip-hop is
bad. The music they used to listen to is horrible.

My mom hardly ever sings. But there she was,
singing that goofball song and dancing around the
living room.

"Come on, Mr. Valentini!" she said, grabbing
Flip's hand. "I took a swing dance class at the Y.
Let's you and me cut a rug, daddy-o!"

Mom and Flip started dancing around the living
room. They were doing the jitterbug or the Charles-
ton, or one of those wacky dances people did a zillion
years ago. It was totally embarrassing. If anybody
from school had been there to see it, I would have
had to pretend I didn't know them.

Fortunately, Flip got winded pretty quickly and
had to sit down on the couch. My mom kept right on
dancing without him.

"So what do you say?" she asked, swirling her dress around. "Can I come to 1942 too? You might need me to sweet talk some of those old baseball players. Or maybe I could drive your getaway car."

"Not this time, Mom," I said. "Flip and I have important baseball research to conduct."

"Oh, pooh on that," Mom said with a pout. "I was hoping I could meet some handsome dreamboat outfielder and we'd run off and live happily ever after. Isn't that the way it always happened back in the 1940s, Mr. Valentini?"

"Uh, not in my case, no," Flip said.

"Well, I packed you some lunch anyway," she said, skipping into the kitchen to get two paper bags from the refrigerator. "And here are some Band-Aids, just in case anything happens."

She is *so* overprotective. Flip put the bags in the suitcase.

"Do you have your baseball cards?" she asked.

That's right! I almost forgot. Besides the Satchel Paige postcard, I needed to bring a *new* baseball card with me too. Just like the 1942 card would take us to 1942, the new card would bring Flip and me back to the present day.

I ran upstairs and grabbed a pack of new cards from my desk drawer. I stuck it in my pants pocket and ran back downstairs to sit on the couch next to Flip. He had the suitcase on his lap now, and the Satchel Paige card was on top of it.

It was time.

"Let's do it," I said.

I took Flip's hand in mine. It was sweaty.

"You nervous?" I asked.

"A little."

"It's gonna be great, Flip. Trust me. I'm getting good at this."

"I hope we don't have to do any runnin'," Flip said. "I don't get around too good anymore. The legs are shot."

"You won't have to run. I promise."

Flip handed me the Satchel Paige card. I closed my eyes and concentrated. "You boys be careful, now," Mom said. "I don't want anything to happen."

"I'm always careful, Mom," I said. "Don't worry. Nothing's going to happen."

"Joey, you take care of Mr. Valentini and do everything he says."

"I will, Mom."

"And Mr. Valentini, you take care of Joey, and don't do *anything* he says."

"Yes, Mrs. Stoshack."

"Please fasten your seat belts and put your tray tables in the upright and locked position," my mother said.

"Mom, I can't concentrate," I said. "Would you mind, uh . . ."

"Okay, okay. I'm leaving!" Mom said. She kissed me on the forehead. "You are such a big boy!"

I heard her footsteps tramp up the stairs. It was quiet. I concentrated on the card in my hand.

"What if something goes wrong?" Flip whispered. "Does anything ever go wrong?"

"Yeah," I said. "Sometimes. Time travel isn't an exact science. You never know where we're gonna wind up or what's gonna happen. Whatever it is, we'll deal with it."

I didn't mention to Flip that something *always* seems to go wrong. In my previous trips through time, I had a nasty habit of attracting gunfire in my direction.

I thought I felt a slight tingle in my fingertips. It might have been a false alarm.

"What if we never come back?" Flip asked.

"Shhh. Just relax," I said.

I could definitely feel that tingling sensation in my fingers that were holding the card.

"But what if we don't?" Flip asked. "You know, 1942 was such a long time ago."

"How old were you back then?" I asked, keeping my eyes closed and focusing on the feeling.

"Lemme see," Flip said. "I was born in 1934. So in 1942 I was . . . eight."

My right arm was tingling now. I could feel the sensation starting to move across my body.

"Do you remember what it felt like to be young?" I asked. Both my arms were tingling now. It was such a pleasant feeling.

"Man, those were the days," Flip said. "It's true what they say, Stosh. Youth is wasted on the young. I sure wish I was young again. Like, say, eighteen.

That was a good age. Boy, if I knew then what I know now, I woulda done things different. I woulda done a lotta things different."

The tingling sensation was sweeping up and down me now, like a wave. My body was almost vibrating. I had reached the point of no return. I wanted to see what it looked like, but I didn't dare open my eyes.

"What would you have done differently?" I asked.

I never heard Flip's response.

I felt myself fading away.

7

The Diner

"NEED SOME KETCHUP AT TABLE THREE!"

"Gimme one Adam and Eve on a raft! Make it to go!"

"One blue plate special! And a hockey puck!"

I opened my eyes. I was sitting at a booth in a diner, with waitresses hustling back and forth and the loud buzz of conversation all around. What a relief! At least I hadn't landed in a dark alley, or in some battlefield with bullets whizzing by my face.

Flip was nowhere to be seen. A teenage kid was sitting on the other side of the table, and he was staring at me.

"Who are you?" I asked him.

"What do you mean, who am I?" the kid replied. "Stosh, it's me!"

"Me who?"

"Flip!"

"Get outta here!" I said.

The kid couldn't have been more than nineteen. Twenty, tops.

"You're not Flip," I said. "Flip is an old man."

I noticed that Flip's suitcase was next to the kid in the booth. He looked at himself in the shiny metal surface of the napkin holder. His jaw dropped open. He touched his face and pulled at his skin as if he didn't think it was real. The kid took off his hat. He had short blond hair.

"Hey, I look *good*!" he said.

The kid was wearing the same clothes as Flip too. And they fit him!

"Where's Flip?" I demanded. "What did you do to him?"

"Stosh, I swear, I *am* Flip."

"Prove it," I said. "Who won the World Series in 1955?"

"The Bums, of course. The Brooklyn Dodgers," he said. "It was the only year they ever won."

"Well, everybody knows that," I said. "That doesn't prove you're Flip."

"We live in Louisville, Kentucky, Stosh," the kid said. "I run a baseball card shop there."

"Oh yeah? Well, why are you called Flip?" I asked.

"When I was a kid, me and my buddies in Brooklyn used to flip baseball cards against the wall. Stosh, you *gotta* believe me. I'm your Little League coach! We came here to see how fast Satchel Paige could throw a ball."

It really *was* Flip! When I looked at his face closely, I could see a slight resemblance. But he was more than fifty years younger than the Flip I knew.

Then I figured out what must have happened. When I travel through time, I get whatever I wish for. One time I wished I was an adult, and when I opened my eyes in 1909, I was a grown man. This time, Flip wished he could be eighteen years old again. And he was!

While I was figuring it all out, Flip took off his jacket. He rolled up a sleeve and made a muscle.

"Hey, Stosh!" he said, admiring his bulging biceps. "Check this out!"

"Okay, okay," I said. "Flip, will you knock that off? People are staring."

I looked around the diner. It had those red stools that spin around. There was a jukebox in the corner. There were a bunch of pies in a glass container on the counter. It was just like one of those diners that are made to look like they're from a long time ago. Only this one really *was* from a long time ago.

"Hey, Flip," I whispered. "Did you see that waitress over there? She's beautiful!"

"Fuhgetabout that, Stosh! What are we doin' here? I thought we were supposed to meet Satchel Paige."

"Be patient," I said. "He might walk in the door any minute. Or we might have to go find him. But believe me, he's around somewhere."

"Somethin' tells me we ain't gonna see Satchel Paige in *this* joint," Flip said.

"Why not?"

Flip pointed to a sign above the restroom door. It said WHITES ONLY. Everybody in the diner was white, I noticed. It never would have occurred to me if I hadn't seen the sign.

"It's the 1940s," Flip said. "It's a different world."

This was a world Flip knew from when he was a kid. He beamed from ear to ear when he saw something he remembered. "Look, Stosh!" he said. "Clicquot Club orange phosphate soda! I used to drink that stuff all the time back in Brooklyn!" He pointed out the old Studebaker and Nash cars through the window.

But mostly, Flip was admiring his new muscles. He was really built, and he kept flexing his arms and posing proudly.

"Will you quit that?" I said, "It's embarrassing, Flip! You're in your seventies."

"Not here I ain't," he said pulling the front of his shirt out of his pants. "Hey, get a load of my abs, Stosh! I got a six-pack!"

Suddenly I noticed somebody was standing next to our table. It was that good-looking waitress. Her name tag read LAVERNE.

"You wanna put your tummy away, big boy?" she said. "This is a family place."

"I'm sorry," said Flip, and his face got all red.

This girl Laverne was *really* cute. She had long dark hair with curled bangs and these piercing green eyes. She was probably the prettiest girl I had ever seen.

"What can I get you fellas?" Laverne asked.

"Oh, we're not hungry," Flip said.

Laverne put a hand on her hip and stared at him.

"Just like sittin' 'round diners?" she asked.

"We were about to leave," Flip said.

I kicked him under the table. He looked at me and I mouthed the words, "She's *hot!*" but he just ignored me. When it came to women, Flip was clueless.

"Sure we're hungry," I said. "What's the specialty of the house?"

"My daddy makes roast chicken and corn bread that will make you think you died and went to heaven," Laverne said.

Through an opening in the back of the diner, I saw a guy cooking on a smoky stove. He was wearing a white apron and one of those white paper hats.

"Do you have anything that's low carb?" Flip asked.

"Low *what?*" Laverne replied, and I kicked Flip under the table again. I'm not even sure they knew what carbohydrates *were* in 1942. Come to think of it, I don't even know what they are *now*.

"The chicken sounds good," I said. "How much is it?"

"For you, a buck and a quarter."

"That's *all*?" I asked.

"You can pay more if you wanna," Laverne said.

"Can I get a Coke too?"

"Sure thing, toots."

"I'll have a cup of coffee," Flip said.

"CUPPA JOE!" Laverne called out toward the kitchen. "How do you like it, handsome?"

"Black," Flip replied.

"NO COW!" Laverne shouted.

"Hey, can I ask you something?" I said.

"Well, you're a little young to be wantin' my telephone number," she replied, glancing at Flip.

"No," I said. "Where *are* we? I mean, what town?"

"Hon, you're right outside the beautiful town of Spartanburg, South Carolina."

"And it's 1942, right?" I asked.

"Last time I looked," Laverne said. "Say, you don't get out much, do ya? I'll be right back with your drinks."

Laverne left and I kicked Flip again.

"Did you see the way she was looking at you?" I asked. "She likes you, Flip. She's flirting!"

"Don't be silly. Waitresses just smile like that to get good tips."

"Yeah, but after we track down Satchel Paige, you should ask her out on a date."

"Stosh, I don't even know her!"

"Well, that's how you'll *get* to know her," I insisted.

I heard a noise outside, so I looked out the window.

A bus had pulled up. The words "Homestead Grays" were painted on the side.

It wasn't long before Laverne came back with our drinks.

"My friend Flip here says you're the prettiest girl he's ever seen," I told her.

"I did not!" Flip exclaimed.

Laverne smiled. "You're pretty cute yourself, Flip." She giggled. "How old are you?"

"Seventy-two," Flip replied.

"Hahahaha! He's joking!" I said. "Flip's eighteen. What a kidder!"

"Well, it just so happens that I'm gonna be eighteen in a couple of days myself," Laverne said. "What do you do, honey?"

"Flip's a baseball player," I said. "He's thinking of trying out for the Dodgers."

"Stosh!" Flip yelled.

"Oh, too bad," Laverne said. "Daddy won't let me go with a ballplayer. He says they're low class."

"Low class?" I said. "Baseball players make millions of dollars a year."

"What planet are *you* from?" Laverne asked.

I glanced up at Laverne's father in the kitchen. He was shooting dirty looks in our direction. Laverne winked at Flip and said she had to take care of another table.

Flip and I were sipping our drinks when I noticed that the diner had suddenly grown quiet. Nobody was talking. Silverware stopped clicking against plates. Nobody was eating. Everybody was looking toward the front door.

An African American kid had just walked in. He looked like he was about my age.

I peeked out the window at the bus parked at the curb. Inside the bus windows, I could see a bunch of black guys. It looked like they were wearing baseball caps.

The kid walked up to the lady at the cash register.

"I'd like to order twenty hamburgers, please," he said.

Laverne's father rushed out of the kitchen.

"I'm sorry, sonny," he said, "but we can't help you. Ain't nothin' personal, you understand. You can use the bathrooms out back if you need 'em."

The kid lowered his head for a moment. It looked like he might cry. He was probably hungry. He just turned around without a word and walked back to the front door.

I got out of my seat and caught up with him before he could leave.

"Hey," I said. "Where's your mother?"

"Ain't got no mother," he told me. "My momma died the day I was born. Daddy takes care of me."

He pointed toward the bus, which was still outside. Then he opened the door and left the diner. When I went back, Flip was standing at the cash register.

"I'd like to order twenty hamburgers," Flip said to Laverne's father. "To go."

Everybody in the diner was staring at Flip.

Laverne's father looked at him. "What are you, a wise guy?" he asked.

"No, I'm a hungry guy," Flip said, "and I'd like twenty burgers. Are you refusing to serve me?"

Laverne's father looked disgusted. He went back to the kitchen and told somebody to put twenty burgers on the grill.

Flip and I sat down again. People were looking at us and whispering. Soon our chicken was done and Laverne came over with the platters. Outside, the engine of the bus started up again.

"Stosh!" Flip said. "Quick, go tell the driver to hold that bus a minute!"

I ran outside. The bus was starting to pull away. I banged on the door. The driver hit the brakes. The door opened.

"Wait!" I yelled.

Flip was jogging out of the diner with the two platters of chicken and the paper bag lunches my mom had packed for us. He climbed up the steps of the bus. I followed. All the guys on the bus were wearing baseball uniforms that said "Grays" across the front.

"Gentlemen," Flip said. "Anybody want some roast chicken and cornbread? Believe me, this stuff is so good, you'll feel like you died and went to heaven. And if you can wait a few minutes, I ordered those burgers you wanted."

For a moment, the ballplayers on the bus just

stared at Flip, like they didn't trust him. But I guess their hunger overwhelmed any suspicions they had, because they all started grabbing the food and shouting. "Yeah! I want some! Gimme a drumstick! What's in the bag? I'll take a hunk of that cornbread. . . ." They dove into the food like they hadn't had a good meal in a long time.

The kid who had come into the diner was sitting in the seat right behind the driver. His eyes were moist with tears.

"What's your name, son?" Flip asked, giving him one of my mom's sandwiches.

"Joshua," the kid said. "Josh Gibson."

I thought Flip was going to fall over. He staggered back a step and his eyes bugged out. He looked like he was about to pass out.

"Josh Gibson . . . the ballplayer?" he asked.

At that, a huge man stepped forward and stuck out his hand for Flip to shake.

"I'm Josh Gibson, the ballplayer," he said. "This is my son, Josh Junior."

The guy was like a mountain. He was about as tall as Flip, but his chest, arms, and legs were enormous. There may have been a little bit of a belly there, but mostly he was solid muscle.

"I want to thank you, mister," he said simply.

"Stosh!" Flip said, pumping the guy's hand, "This is the great Josh Gibson. The Bronzed Bambino. Prob'bly the greatest hitter in baseball history. Hey Josh, is it true you hit 84 homers in 1936? Is it true you batted .600 one year? I heard you hit line drives that tear the gloves off infielders."

"It's true," Gibson sighed. "All of it."

The greatest hitter in baseball history? I had never even heard of him. I looked at Josh Gibson more closely. His eyes looked weary. There was a sadness in them.

"Numbers don't mean nothin'," one of the other players said. "I remember this one time we were playin' in Pittsburgh and Josh hit one outta sight. Looked like it was *never* gonna come down. The next day we were playin' in Philly and this ball comes flying out of the sky. Somebody caught it and the ump says to Josh, 'Yer out! Yesterday, in Pittsburgh!'"

Everybody cracked up. Josh Gibson introduced some of the other players. When he said this one guy's name was Cool Papa Bell, Flip just about fainted again. Bell was another famous player from the Negro Leagues who I hadn't heard of.

"Is Satchel Paige here?" I asked.

The players all started laughing, like I had told a joke or something.

"Satchel Paige don't play for the Homestead Grays," the boy said. "He plays for the Kansas City Monarchs. Everybody knows that."

Well, I didn't know that.

"Tell me," Flip asked, "is Paige as fast as they say he is?"

"Fast?" Josh Gibson said. "Me and Satch used to be teammates on the Pittsburgh Crawfords. I was his catcher for five years. And believe me, nobody can fish like Satch, nobody can flap his gums like Satch, and *nobody* is faster than Satch. Greatest pitcher I ever seen."

"Satch throws fire, that's what he throws!" added Cool Papa Bell.

"It's like he winds up with a pumpkin and he throws you a pea," somebody else added.

Cool Papa Bell

"Oh, I'm gonna take care of Satch and his big mouth when we meet up in Pittsburgh, believe you me," Josh said. "I'm gonna shut him up."

"You're playin' the Monarchs in Pittsburgh soon?" asked Flip, throwing me a look.

"You got that right, mister," Cool Papa Bell said. "We're on our way there now."

Laverne came out of the diner with a big platter piled high with burgers. The players looked at her like they'd never seen a pretty girl before. She seemed hesitant to step inside the bus, so Flip took the platter from her.

"Daddy says these fellas are welcome to eat here," she told Flip, "so long as they don't come in the restaurant."

"Thank you kindly, miss," Flip said.

The players started pulling out money to give to Flip, but he wouldn't take it. "Lunch is on me, guys," he said, passing out the burgers. Grateful hands reached out to grab them.

Flip signaled for me that we should go, but Josh Gibson invited us to stay until they had to get back on the road. The seats were all filled, so we stood.

"Hey, I'm sorry about what happened in there," Flip told them.

"Ain't your fault," Josh said, biting into a burger. "Ain't nobody's fault."

In school I had learned a little bit about the prejudice and discrimination that took place in

America before the civil rights movement. I had also taken a time travel trip to see Jackie Robinson become the first black major leaguer in sixty years. Seeing bigotry with my own eyes made it more real. It was so unfair. I couldn't imagine how anybody, black or white, could put up with it.

"Aren't you mad?" I asked.

"What's the use?" Gibson said. "Ain't nothin' we can do about people who don't like us. What are we gonna do? Write to our congressmen?"

"Son, we're just tryin' to survive," said Cool Papa Bell. "Put food on the table."

"I heard the Red Sox are gonna hold tryouts for Negro players," one of the other players said.

"Oh, that's just talk," said Gibson.

"Someday there'll be black players in the big leagues," I told them. I didn't want to tell them I was from the future, but I wanted to give them hope.

"Yeah, well, someday ain't today," said Bell.

"I'll believe it when I see it," somebody else added.

"In a few years—," I started.

"Son, I'm thirty years old," interrupted Josh Gibson. "Cool Papa here is thirty-nine. In a few years, it'll be too late for us."

"Where are you staying tonight?" Flip asked, changing the subject.

"There's a hotel an hour or so north of here,"

Gibson said. "We hear they take in colored folks. If not, we'll have to sleep on the bus, like last night."

What a rotten life. They can't just walk into any restaurant and sit at a table, like I can. They can't just pull into a hotel and expect to get a room. They have to sleep and eat and ride all day on a crummy bus.

"Why do you do it?" I asked Josh Gibson.

"I guess we just love playin' ball," he said.

Flip motioned again that we should go. We got off the bus and the driver gunned the engine. Before the bus pulled away, Josh Gibson came out and shook Flip's hand again.

"Thank you kindly for the food," he said.

"Fuhgetaboutit," Flip replied. "Hey, you think Satch and the Monarchs will be passing through this way?"

"Sooner or later," Josh said, "most everybody comes this way."

He climbed back inside the bus and it pulled away.

Flip and I watched until the bus disappeared down the road.

"I guess we've got to get to Pittsburgh," I said.

"I'll get my suitcase."

When we walked back in the diner, Laverne's father was behind the cash register. He looked at us with disgust and handed something to Flip. It was a bill. All the food we ordered only came to seventeen dollars. Flip patted his pockets until he found his wallet. He opened it up.

Flip's wallet was empty.

"Uh, Stosh, you got any money on you?"

8

Thumbing a Ride

SEVENTEEN DOLLARS.

It really doesn't sound like that much money. I guess if you happen to have a thousand dollars in your pocket, seventeen isn't very much at all. But when you have *nothing* in your pocket and you're in a different century and there's this mean-looking guy holding his hand out and demanding money, it's another story.

Suddenly, seventeen dollars seemed like a fortune.

"You don't have any money?" I whispered to Flip.

"I forgot all about bringing money," Flip said, panic creeping into his voice. "I didn't think I'd need any."

"What's your name, boy?" Laverne's father suddenly asked.

"Stosh," I said. "Joe Stoshack."

"Not *you*!" he said. "The big guy. What's *your* name?"

"Flip Valentini, sir. We're just, uh . . ."

"Valentini, eh?" Laverne's father muttered. "You an Italian?"

He said the word like *Eye*-talian.

"Yes, sir," Flip said. He was being especially polite.

Laverne's father made a face. It didn't look like he liked Italians any better than blacks. He didn't look like he liked *anybody*.

I don't always carry money with me, but I patted my pocket and breathed a sigh of relief that my wallet was in there. I still had the twenty-dollar bill I would have used if Flip hadn't outbid me on the eBay auction. I handed it to Laverne's father.

"Lunch is on me," I said. I'd always wanted to say, "Lunch is on me." It made me feel like a big shot.

Laverne's father took my bill and looked at it.

"This is a fake!" he said. "This ain't no real twenty! Look at that. Andrew Jackson's head is too big, and it ain't in the middle!"

"It's not fake!" I said, "It's—"

What was I supposed to say? That the bill was printed in the twenty-first century and I traveled back through time with it?

"It's a new bill, sir," Flip said. "Just issued."

"You two are counterfeiters!" Laverne's father shouted. Then he took my bill and ripped it in half.

"Hey!" I yelled. "That's perfectly good money!"

"Tell it to the cops," Laverne's father said. He

was reaching for the phone on the counter. Flip put his hand over the phone.

"No need to call the police, sir," Flip said, forcing a laugh. "We were just kiddin' with that bill. Do you accept American Express cards?"

"American Express?" asked Laverne's father. "What's that?"

"Look, I'll write you a check," Flip said.

"I ain't takin' your damn check!" said Laverne's father. "You try to pass counterfeit dough and you think I'm gonna take your *check*? I accept cash, son. Cold, hard cash. If you ain't got none, I got a lotta dishes in the back that need washin'."

"You wouldn't by any chance have an ATM here, would you?" I asked.

"A *what*?"

Laverne's dad grabbed Flip by the arm and pulled him into the kitchen. I followed. There was a huge sink back there. It looked more like a bathtub. Dishes and pots were piled up higher than my head.

"Start scrubbin'," Laverne's father said. "And they better be squeaky clean, or you're gonna have to do 'em all over again."

Laverne's dad went back to his grill on the other side of the kitchen. That's when I got a great idea. We didn't have to wash these stupid dishes. We could just take my new pack of baseball cards and get *out* of there. Go home. Back to our own century. We didn't need this aggravation.

But Flip wouldn't go for it. When I told him about my brainstorm, he said that wouldn't be right. We had ordered seventeen dollars' worth of food, and we had to pay for seventeen dollars' worth of food. If we didn't have the money, the right thing to do would be to wash the dishes.

"We had the money!" I said. "He ripped up my twenty-dollar bill!"

"I'll wash," Flip said. "You dry."

That's one thing about Flip that drives me crazy. He *always* has to do the right thing.

Flip put on a pair of yellow rubber gloves and grabbed a big hunk of steel wool. I picked up a towel. We got to work.

It felt like it took a year, but it was probably only an hour or two. I felt sorry for Flip. The pots were caked with food and grease and crud and who knows what. It was disgusting. I made a mental note to be sure to go to college so I wouldn't have to grow up and wash dishes for a living.

We were about halfway done when Laverne suddenly poked her head into the sink area. She looked around to make sure her father didn't see her. Flip tried to fix his hair, but he had soap on his rubber glove and all he accomplished was putting some bubbles on the top of his head. He was pretty funny looking.

"I'm sorry about Daddy," Laverne said. "Sometimes he's . . ."

"It's okay," Flip said. "It's not your fault."

"Listen," Laverne said, "I just wanted to tell you boys that was a kind thing you did out there for the colored men on the bus."

"It was all Flip's idea," I said.

"Well, I think you're very brave," she said, reaching up and brushing some bubbles off Flip's hair.

"It was nothin'," Flip said. His face was all red.

"Are you gonna be in town for a while?" Laverne asked.

"Nah," Flip said. "We're heading for Pittsburgh."

"Pittsburgh!" she said. "Lordy, that's five hundred miles away! I wish I could see a big city like Pittsburgh."

"We're going to see Satchel Paige pitch," I added.

"Where's Laverne?" her father suddenly shouted from the dining room. "We got customers waitin' out here!"

Laverne quickly reached into her apron and pulled out a handful of change.

"Here," she said, pressing the coins into Flip's hand. "You'll need money to get to Pittsburgh."

Laverne scurried away. Flip put the money in his pocket and grabbed the next pot to wash.

"Flip!" I said. "She's crazy about you! That's her tip money. You gotta ask her out, man!"

"Stosh, that girl is seventeen years old," Flip said. "I'm seventy-two!"

"Not here you aren't!" I insisted. "If you don't ask her out, I'm going to come back in five years when I'm eighteen and ask her out myself."

"You do that, Stosh."

Poor Flip. When it came to women, he just didn't know what to say or do. He got all shy and nervous. I told him he should just be himself and talk to Laverne. You know, ask her what she likes to do. Make conversation. Flip said he'd think about it. There was just no talking sense to him.

By the time we emptied the sink of pots and pans, Flip and I were exhausted. Laverne's father came out while I was drying the last pot.

"Okay, you boys can go now," he said gruffly. "But I don't want to see you two 'round here no more, y'hear me? I don't need your business. And I don't need your colored friends' business neither."

"Yes, sir," Flip said. He grabbed his suitcase and we left the diner. I looked around to say good-bye to Laverne, but she was nowhere in sight.

It was late afternoon by this time. The lunch crowd was gone and there weren't many cars on the street outside the diner.

"How are we gonna get to Pittsburgh?" I asked Flip.

"Only way we can," he said. Flip walked over to the side of the road and stuck out his thumb.

My mother once told me that I should *never* hitchhike. She said that getting into a car with a stranger is really dangerous. You don't know what kind of lunatic might pick you up. But Flip said that back in the old days, people hitchhiked all the time.

It was safer back then. Not as many people owned cars. There was no other way for some people to get around. And maybe there weren't as many lunatics running around back in the 1940s.

We walked down the road in the same direction the Homestead Grays' bus had been going. Every so often we'd turn around if we heard a car coming. Then we'd stick out our thumbs. Flip told me to look sad and pathetic so people would feel sorry for us and stop to pick us up. It wasn't hard to do. We *were* sad and pathetic.

But nobody even slowed down for us. Ten or twenty cars must have passed by, and all they did was leave us in a cloud of dust. It was depressing. I told Flip we should just forget about this whole silly idea of clocking Satchel Paige. I had a fresh pack of baseball cards in my pocket. We could go back home anytime we wanted.

"Let's just wait for a few more cars," Flip said.

And that's when I saw it.

"Look! A bus!" I shouted.

In the distance, I could see a gray bus coming our way. Maybe it was going to Pittsburgh. We wouldn't even have to hitchhike. We had the money Laverne had given us. We could use it to pay the bus fare.

The bus got closer and we waved our hands in the air to let the driver know we wanted to get on.

"He's not slowin' down," Flip said.

Flip was right. The bus was going about 50 miles

an hour, and it was almost on top of us. I could see some lettering on the side. It read:

KANSAS CITY MONARCHS

"Wait!" I screamed as the bus blew past us. "Stop!"

No use. The bus kept right on going.

"Satchel Paige plays for the Monarchs!" I shouted to Flip. "He's on that bus!"

The bus was gone. Flip put his suitcase on the ground at the side of the road and sat down on it. He took off his hat and wiped his forehead.

"Well, we tried," he said wearily. "We gave it our best shot. Let's go home, Stosh."

I sat down next to him. We were both depressed. I pulled out my pack of new baseball cards and ripped off the wrapper. I took out one of the cards and put the rest back in my pocket. Flip grabbed my hand.

"Close your eyes," I said.

We closed our eyes and I concentrated. I imagined us in the twenty-first century again. Back in Louisville. Home. It wasn't long until I started to feel the slightest tingle in my fingertips.

As we sat there, I heard a car engine in the distance. It got louder, so I knew it was getting closer. I ignored it. Flip and I had resigned ourselves to the fact that we weren't going to make it to Pittsburgh. We just wanted to get out of there.

The tingling sensation had moved up my arm when the car skidded to a halt right in front of us. I heard the door open, and then shut. Somebody got out of the car. There were footsteps on the gravel.

I opened my eyes. There was a tall black man sitting on the front bumper of the car. He was lighting a cigarette.

"Who are you?" I asked.

"Name's Leroy," the man said. "But most folks call me Satch. You fellas need a lift?"

I dropped the card.

This is what I saw when I opened my eyes.

9

Satch

"YOU BOYS LOOK SADDER THAN A POLECAT STUCK UP a tree."

It was him! The real Satchel Paige! He was right in front of us! In the flesh! I could have reached out and touched him.

We didn't have to give this guy a quiz to make him prove he was really Satchel Paige. He looked just like he did in photos. He had these droopy eyelids and smooth dark skin. He had a look like a basset hound.

It works, I reminded myself. Every time I travel through time, I land in the year on the card. I may not land right next to the person I'm trying to meet, but one way or another, I'm always able to find my way to the guy. How could I have ever doubted myself?

I looked over at Flip. He was just staring at Satchel Paige with his mouth open.

"We're not sad," I said. "We're just so surprised to see you, Mr. Paige. Surprised and happy."

He wasn't wearing a baseball uniform. He was all dressed up in a snazzy suit, wide-brimmed hat, and shiny shoes.

He got up off the bumper and came over to shake hands with us. Satchel Paige was tall, about six foot four. He looked like a big gooney bird, or a scarecrow. His string bean arms and legs seemed to go on forever. He was so skinny you wondered what held his pants up. But his feet were enormous.

He was a sight, I'll tell you that much. I tried not to stare, but I couldn't help it.

"Call me Satch," he said.

When we shook hands, his fingers wrapped around mine like an octopus. I had never seen such long fingers before. Fingers like that could give a baseball a lot of backspin. Put a lot of hop on a fastball. Put a lot of break on a curve.

"Joe Stoshack," I said. "My friends call me Stosh. And this is my friend Flip Valentini."

Flip still hadn't said anything. It was like he was in a daze. He kept shaking until Satch pulled his hand away.

"Does your friend talk?" Satch asked. "Or is he one of them deaf-mutes?"

"Nice car," Flip croaked. "Is that a Packard?"

The car was bright red, and shiny. It was rounded on all the edges, the way cars used to be a long time ago.

"Yup, 1940," Satch said. "This baby can really scoot. Just about rubbed the paint off, polishin' her so much. Used to belong to Bette Davis, y'know."

"Who's Bette Davis?" I asked, and Satch looked at me strangely.

"She's a movie star," Flip told me.

"Say, where are you fellas from?" Satch asked.

"Louisville, Kentucky," I said. I had the feeling that Satch was sizing us up to see if it was safe to let us in his car.

"And you hitched all the way from Louisville?"

I didn't know what to say. I've never been a very good liar. Luckily, Flip bailed me out.

"We took the bus most of the way," he said. "We're down to our last five bucks. We've been washin' dishes to pay for food."

"I been there," Satch said. "Where are you boys headin'?"

Flip and I looked at each other. The only place we were heading was wherever Satchel Paige was heading.

"Pittsburgh," we said at the same time.

"Just so happens I'm headin' to Smoketown myself," Satch said. "I reckon you boys look like fine upstandin' citizens. You're welcome to accompany me, if you don't mind makin' a stop or two 'long the way."

"That'll be fine!" Flip said.

Satch opened the door and I got in the backseat. Flip grabbed his suitcase, but when he picked it up by the handle, it opened. He must have clicked the latches accidentally when he was sitting on it.

When the suitcase opened, the radar gun fell out and landed in the grass.

"What's that thing you got there?" Satch asked.

Flip and I looked at each other.

"You'd never believe us," I said.

"Try me," said Satch. "I seen it all."

"It's a radar gun," Flip said. "It uses microwaves."

"Microwaves?" Satch said.

There was no point in lying. I decided just to tell him the truth.

"Satch," I explained, "Flip and I don't live in 1942. We live in the twenty-first century. You see, I have the power to use baseball cards to travel through time."

Flip shook his head, like he couldn't believe I would be so dumb as to tell Satchel Paige the truth about us. But what was I supposed to say? How could I explain this machine that wouldn't exist for thirty years?

"I heard taller tales than that one," Satch said. "What can you shoot at with that thing?"

"You don't shoot *at* anything," Flip said. "It tracks the speed of moving objects."

There was a car coming down the road from the right. Flip turned on the radar gun and pointed it at the car as it passed by. The little screen on the back of the gun flashed "38."

"That car is goin' 38 miles an hour," Flip said.

"It's digital," I added. Satch let out a whistle.

"Lucky the police don't have one of those," he marveled. "I'd be in *big* trouble."

Flip and I looked at each other again. There was no point in telling Satch that someday the police *would* have radar guns.

"Can that thing track a bird?" Satch asked.

"I guess so," Flip said. He pointed the gun up in the air. A few seconds went by before a bird flew overhead. The little screen on the gun flashed "31."

"Never seen nothin' like that!" Satch said.

He helped Flip close his suitcase and we piled in the car. Flip got in the passenger seat. Satch put the key in the ignition, but he stopped before turning it.

"Say," he said to Flip, "can you track a baseball with that thing?"

"That's exactly what it's made for," Flip said. "In fact, we came here to see how fast you throw."

"Well, I just might break that contraption," Satch said, "'cause nobody can throw a ball as fast as old Satch. Shucks, I'm the fastest there ever was. Fastest there ever will be. Don't let anybody tell you different. Does that thing go up to 100 miles an hour?"

"It sure does," Flip said.

"Faster?" Satch asked.

"Yup," said Flip. "Why don't we find a ballfield and see how fast you throw?"

"My thinkin' precisely," Satch said.

He turned the key and the engine roared to life.

He gunned the accelerator a few times before shifting the car into gear.

"You say you're from the future?" he asked.

"That's right," Flip said.

"Well, that's where I want to go," Satch said. "The future. Maybe that gun of yours can help me get there. But first I got a business meetin' to attend to in Pittsburgh."

"A business meeting?" I asked.

"I got me a business meetin' with Josh Gibson and the Homestead Grays," he said. "We're playin' in the World Series."

He hit the gas, the wheels spun on the dirt, and we roared off down the road.

10

On the Road

THE WORLD SERIES?

Why would Satchel Paige be playing the World Series? I don't know as much baseball history as Flip does, but I do know that Jackie Robinson's rookie year was 1947, and this was only 1942. Satch *couldn't* be in the World Series.

"Is there a World Series in the Negro League?" Flip asked.

I didn't even know that the Negro League had a pennant race. It wasn't mentioned in my baseball books at home.

"Guess they didn't tell you much about *our* league, huh?" Satch asked.

"Not much," I admitted.

The car was bumping along a dirt road, and the needle on the speedometer was just about touching 50.

"You fellas need a little history lesson," Satch

said. "The Homestead Grays topped the National League in '37, '38, '39, '40, '41, and '42. We won the American League pennant in '39, '40, '41, and '42. But there ain't been a World Series 'tween the leagues since '27. So this is it. The best against the best to see who's best."

Satch was driving just a *little* too fast. The road was usually paved, but it wasn't like a highway. I didn't even know if highways existed in 1942. Satch was taking back roads. Making U-turns across pedestrian islands didn't bother him, and he thought nothing of going the wrong way down a one-way street and zigzagging around the oncoming cars.

Flip was in the front seat, and he was gripping the seat like it was a life raft. Forget about airbags, padded dashboards, and safety glass. This car didn't even have seat belts. I guess when cars crashed back in the old days, people just went flying through windshields.

"Slow down!" Flip finally barked, and Satch eased off the gas a little.

It didn't look like he was in a big hurry. This was just the way he drove. Once I was in a car driven by Babe Ruth, and he was even worse. But that's another story.

"How come you don't take the bus with the rest of the Monarchs?" Flip asked.

"I ain't gonna beg some fleabag hotel to let me sleep in their bed," Satch said. "I ain't gonna beg some greasy-spoon restaurant to let me eat their food. I sleep where I want and I eat where I want. I get my own food. I got my dignity. Besides, I like to fly free. I ain't one for the settled-down life. A man rusts sittin' in one spot."

We had come to a stop sign in a little town. There was a row of stores on the left side of the street. A sign on one of them read:

IMPERIAL LAUNDRY COMPANY
WE WASH FOR WHITE PEOPLE ONLY

"I see what you mean," Flip said.

"Are you boys *really* from the future?" Satch suddenly asked after we had passed through the town. "You got television in the future? I heard about television, but I ain't seen one yet."

"Oh yeah," I told him. "We've got wide-screen TVs and DVDs and digital cameras and video games—"

"Here's somethin' you can take back with you to the future," Satch interrupted. "This one game we were leadin' 1–0 in the ninth, and they had runners on first and third. Nobody out. Full count on the batter."

"You were pitching?" Flip asked.

"Not yet," Satch said. "But they called me in to put out the fire. Well, I didn't have my good stuff that day, and I knew it. If you can't overpower 'em, you outcute 'em. So I had to use psychiatry. I come out of the bull pen with a ball hidden in my glove.

The manager handed me the game ball. So now I got two balls in my glove."

"What did you do with them?" Flip asked, snickering. Flip loves those old baseball stories. He eats that stuff up.

"So I go into my windup," Satch said, "and I throw both balls at the same time. One to first and one to third. I picked off both runners, and my motion was so good, the batter took a swing, and he struck out too!"

"Triple play!" Flip said, collapsing with laughter. "Game over!"

"If you can't strike 'em out, you gotta psych 'em out," Satch said.

It occurred to me that Satch didn't care about TV or the technology we would have in the future. He cared about how history was going to remember him.

Major league players got written up in the newspapers every day, even back in the 1940s. Their statistics and accomplishments were preserved for posterity. But Negro League players must have been ignored. Nobody knew what they did. No white people, anyway.

Satch wanted to be remembered. That's what he meant when he said the radar gun could take him to the future. If we returned to the twenty-first century and told everybody that he could throw a baseball faster than anyone, he would go down in history.

"How about pulling over and we'll see how fast you throw?" Flip suggested again.

"Yeah," Satch said, "soon's I find the right spot."

We climbed up a short mountain road, and Satch didn't seem to want to take his foot off the gas, even though the wheels were skidding around the hairpin turns. One slip and the car would go sliding off the side of the mountain.

"How did you get the name Satchel?" Flip asked, once the road finally leveled off.

"I grew up in Mobile, Alabama," he said, "with twelve brothers and sisters. My momma took in washing. We didn't have no money. I used to go down to the train station and carry people's satchels for 'em. Ten cents a satchel. That was good money back then. Anyways, I got me a bright idea. You always got to be thinking if you wanna make money. I got a pole and rope so I could sling three or four satchels together and carry 'em all at one time. Looked like a big old satchel tree. So folks started callin' me Satchel."

I could tell that Flip was filing this stuff in his brain. He was having the time of his life. I was so glad I took him with me.

"We bumped into Josh Gibson and the Homestead Grays before we met up with you," Flip told Satch. The road was winding through woods now.

"That a fact?"

"Josh said he's gonna shut your big mouth in Pittsburgh," I blurted out.

"Stosh!" said Flip.

"That what Josh said?" Satch threw back his head

and let out a good laugh. "I'm the best pitcher in baseball, and Josh is the best hitter. When we played together on the Crawfords, me and Josh always said we'd like to face off in a big game one day with the bases loaded. That would be somethin' to see."

"What do you think would happen?" Flip asked.

"Don't rightly know," Satch said. "But I'll tell you this. Josh can't hit what Josh can't see."

Suddenly, without any warning, Satch slammed on the brakes and the car screeched to a stop. I almost went flying into the front seat, and Flip nearly banged his head on the windshield.

"What's the matter?" Flip yelled. "Did you hit something?"

"Not yet," Satch said, pushing open the door. He ran out of the car and around the back to open the trunk.

"What's he doin'?" Flip asked.

"Beats me."

The next thing we knew, Satch was running off into the woods, and he had a rifle in his hand! Flip and I jumped out of the car and followed him.

"Where's he going?" I yelled to Flip.

"Maybe he's goin' crazy," Flip replied.

We finally caught up with Satch, hiding behind a bush next to a bubbling stream. He was taking aim with the rifle.

"What is it?" I asked.

"Dinner," Satch whispered, not taking his eyes off his target.

I looked off in the distance where he was pointing the gun, and I could see what he was aiming at. It was a deer. A beautiful white-tailed deer, standing motionless in the forest. It must have been about a hundred yards away.

"Are you gonna kill it, Satch?" I asked.

"Darn tootin' I am."

Now, I have mixed feelings about hunting. I mean, it's not like I'm a vegetarian or anything. I eat hamburgers. I eat steak. I don't mind animals being killed for food. I just don't particularly like watching it happen.

Satch pulled the trigger and *bam!*

He missed. Startled by the noise, the deer dashed off into the woods.

"Shoot!" Satch said. "Woulda had 'im if I was throwin' a ball."

We went back to the car so Satch could put his gun away. You should have seen the trunk of that Packard. He kept food and a portable stove in there. There was a heat lamp, an electric massager, and a ukelele. Bats, balls, a couple of gloves, and catcher's equipment. Then there were his clothes. He had a bunch of suits, shirts, and at least two dozen ties. I don't know how all that stuff fit in there.

"What's this?" Flip asked, picking up a pair of red-and-yellow-flowered shorts. They looked like they were made from silk or something.

"Those are my underdrawers, thank you very much," Satch said, snatching them away.

The trunk of the car looked like somebody's closet. I suppose that made sense, because Satch seemed to live in his car.

"I'm starved," Satch said, taking a fishing pole out of the back of the trunk. "You boys up for chow?"

Now that he mentioned it, there was that empty feeling in my stomach. The whole time Flip and I spent at that diner, I never did get anything to eat. We had given all our food to Josh Gibson and the Homestead Grays.

"Aren't you afraid you'll be late for the World Series?" Flip asked. "The Monarchs' bus must be miles ahead of us by now."

"Don't you worry 'bout that," Satch said. "They can't start the game without me. That's why they call it the startin' pitcher, right?"

Satch pulled out his stove and told us to make a fire. He grabbed the fishing pole and a bag and went back into the woods. I gathered some sticks and wood that were lying around under a tree. Flip built the fire. It couldn't have been more than fifteen minutes when Satch came back with a bag of fish.

"Catfish!" Satch said. "Oh, we're gonna eat good tonight!"

Flip offered to cook, but Satch said nobody cooks catfish like he does. He gutted each fish in a few seconds, and then he pulled all kinds of spices and sauces out of the trunk. Soon the smell of roasting fish had my mouth watering. Satch cooked up some potatoes too, which he had stashed in another box.

The food was truly excellent. Flip told Satch that if he ever stopped playing baseball, he could make a good living as a chef.

"Oh, I don't know 'bout that," Satch said, scraping the last of the potatoes off his plate. "Maybe I'll pitch forever. I pitched over a thousand games already, you know."

"A thousand?" I asked. That was hard to believe.

"I won 31 games in 1933," he said, leaning back against a tree. "Threw 64 scoreless innings. Once I won 21 games in a row."

"I didn't know that," Flip said, and he knew just about everything there was to know about baseball.

"Nobody knows," Satch said sadly. "I feel like the majors is a big old house, and it's Christmas mornin' and there are presents everywhere. And I got my nose pressed against the window lookin' in."

"The major league record is 24 wins in a row," Flip said. "Carl Hubbell."

"Major league record?" Satch spit on the grass. "Major league records don't mean nothin,' 'cause I ain't in the major leagues. I don't wanna sound big-headed, but if I was up there, they'd have to rewrite that record book, and you better believe it."

"You're gonna get in the majors, Satch," Flip said. "I can tell you that for sure."

"Well, they better hurry up," Satch said. "I'm just prayin' I get to the big show before my speedball loosens."

"How old are you, Satch?" I asked.

"Don't rightly know," he replied. "My momma told me she kept my birth certificate in the family Bible. But then the house burned down. I'm guessin' I'm 'bout thirty-six, give or take a few."

Satch got up and dusted himself off. He went to the trunk and came back with his ukelele. It was dark out now. I was really tired.

"All this talk is depressin'," Satch said. "How about a song?"

"Sounds good to me," said Flip.

"And you ain't even heard my melodious voice yet," he replied.

Satch strummed the uke and then he started to sing, "'Let me call you sweetheart, I'm in love with you. . . .'"

He could really sing and play! Forget about becoming a chef, I told Satch. He should become a musician.

I can't tell you which songs he played or how long he played or anything like that. Because in the middle of Satch's little concert, I fell asleep right there in the grass.

11

Catching Satch

THUD!

That was the sound my head made when it whacked against the front seat of Satch's car. I had fallen off the backseat when Satch hit the brakes. That woke me up fast. Flip told me I'd slept so soundly that he and Satch had to pick me up off the grass in the middle of the night and throw me in the backseat of the car.

I felt like I had slept a hundred years. It was daytime now. Flip was in the front seat. I was groggy, like I had jet lag. In a way, I did.

"Where are we?" I asked when Satch turned off the engine. "Is this Pittsburgh?"

"Good mornin'," Satch said. "No, we are in the great state of North Carolina."

I sat up and looked out the window. We had pulled off the road at the edge of a field. Some cows were grazing in the distance.

"Why'd you stop here, Satch?" Flip asked.

"I feel like throwin' some," he replied. "Why don't you crank up that gun of yours, and we'll see how high she goes?"

"Sure thing!" I yelled, hopping out of the car. I wasn't groggy anymore. This was the whole reason why I came.

Satch got out and opened the trunk. He took off his fancy clothes and folded them up neatly. He really *did* wear red-and-yellow-flowered underwear!

You would think that a guy who can throw a baseball so hard would have tremendous arm muscles. But when Satch took off his shirt, he seemed to have no muscles at *all*. His arms were unbelievably long. His right arm must be like a slingshot, I figured, with rubber bands instead of muscles.

Satch rooted around in the trunk until he pulled out a jar. There was no label on it. He unscrewed the top and scooped out some brown gooey stuff with two fingers. Then he rubbed the stuff on his pitching arm.

"What's that?" I asked.

"My secret weapon," Satch said, "Venezuelan snake oil."

The stuff smelled horrible.

"I discovered it when I was playin' in Bismarck, North Dakota, in '35," Satch went on. "There were these Sioux Indians up there, and I got to know 'em real good. One day I had a sore arm and I couldn't play. These Indians invited me to their reservation. Well, one of 'em got bit on the leg by a snake and he's rollin' 'round like he's gonna die. The medicine man pulls out some goop and rubs it on the leg to take away the hurt. That put me to thinkin'. I asked him if he could rub some of the stuff on my arm. He said no, it's only for snake bites. So I give him ten American dollars and he rubs some on my arm."

"What happened?" Flip asked.

"Well, my arm got all warm and twitchy," Satch said. "It didn't hurt no more. The next day I went out there and pitched me a no-hitter. That's the truth. So I bought a bucket of the stuff from him, and I dab some on before every game. Keeps my arm young."

"What's in it?" I asked. "It smells disgusting."

"It's a secret formula," Satch said. "The medicine man would only tell me he scoops water out of a hollow tree stump in the woods."

"If you were in North Dakota, why is it called Venezuelan snake oil?" Flip asked.

Satch stopped rubbing the stuff on his arm and thought about it for a moment.

"Maybe it was Venezuela where it happened," he said. "I don't rightly remember. Grab that catcher's gear, Stosh. Let's see if you can catch my speedball."

I was beginning to think that half the stories Satch told he just made up for the fun of it. But I didn't care. Finally we were going to see how fast he really was.

Flip got out the radar gun. I took a catcher's mitt, mask, and chest protector out of the trunk and started putting everything on. The mitt was a fat, round little saucer with a pocket about the size of a ball. It didn't look anything like the catcher's mitts I had used. He didn't have any shin guards.

Satch finished rubbing on that evil-smelling snake oil. He pulled a baseball uniform out of the trunk and put it on. Spikes too.

The uniform said NEW YORK STARS across the front. When I asked him why it wasn't a Kansas City Monarchs uniform, he said that sometimes he pitched for the Monarchs, sometimes he pitched for the Stars, and sometimes he pitched for other teams.

"I play for whoever pays," he said. "When the green's floatin' 'round, make sure you get your share."

The three of us hopped a wooden fence and went out into the field. Satch found a bump that looked a little like a pitching mound. He paced off sixty feet and six inches and put a chewing-gum wrapper on the ground there.

"You squat down right behind that," he said.

"*That's* home plate?" I asked. "It's a little small, don't you think?"

"Don't you worry 'bout a thing," Satch said. "I can hit a butterfly with a clamshell."

Satch went back to the "mound" and swung his arm around a few times.

"Never do nothin' till your muscles are all loosed up," he said.

I squatted behind the "plate." Flip stood a few feet behind me with the radar gun and pointed it toward Satch.

This was the moment. We weren't just going to witness history, we were going to *make* history.

I was a little nervous. I'm pretty good with the glove, but I had never caught anyone who threw really hard. Satch himself said that Josh Gibson wouldn't be able to hit what he couldn't see. What if I couldn't see the ball coming at me? I made sure the catcher's mask was strapped on tight.

"I'll start you off nice and slow and easy," Satch said.

I put the mitt up and got ready to receive the pitch. I watched his motion carefully so I'd see the ball the whole way. He brought his arms high over his head really slowly, kicked up his leg, and—

I never saw the ball. It just exploded in the mitt like it had been sent to me electronically. It felt like a bomb went off in my hand. Tears came to my eyes.

"75 miles per hour," shouted Flip.

Only 75? It felt like the ball must have been going 100 miles an hour.

"You okay, Stosh?" Flip asked.

"Yeah."

No way I was going to let them know how much my hand hurt. I threw the ball back to Satch.

He caught it and wound up again. I braced

myself for the impact. The ball made a weird humming noise after he released it, and it exploded in the mitt again. I didn't have to move it an inch.

"81 miles per hour," Flip called.

That one didn't hurt as much as the first one. Maybe it was because I was ready for it. Or maybe it was because my hand was so numb I couldn't feel anything. I threw the ball back to Satch.

He let another one fly. Again, it hit the center of the mitt. The guy had incredible control.

"89 miles per hour," Flip called. "Is that your fastest, Satch?"

"Not even close," Satch replied, winding up for another one. It smacked into the mitt like a freight train.

"94 miles per hour," Flip called. "You think you can break 100?"

"Piece of cake," Satch replied, grabbing my return throw and immediately winding up for another one. "I ain't even hit the gas yet."

My legs were getting tired from squatting. My hand was killing me from the pounding it had taken. But I wasn't complaining. I was going to catch the fastest pitch ever thrown. How many other kids could say that?

Satch let another one loose and it popped into the mitt.

"99 miles per hour," Flip called out excitedly.

I returned the ball to Satch. This was it. He was throwing harder with each pitch. The next one was sure to crack 100 miles per hour, and who knows how much faster Satch could throw? Maybe he could hit 105 . . . 110 even.

"Your hand okay?" Satch yelled.

"It feels great!" I lied. "Is that all you got?"

"Burn it in, Satch!" hollered Flip. "Stosh can take it."

Satch went into his windup. He was about to bring that whip of an arm down.

Bam!

It was a blast. A gunshot. I heard a bullet ricochet off a tree. Satch never even let go of the ball.

"Drop that gun, sonny!" somebody yelled.

12

The Clowns

THE THREE OF US FROZE.

I really wanted to find out whether or not Satch could break 100 miles per hour on the radar gun. But staying alive seemed like a pretty good idea too. I looked around, but I couldn't see the guy who had shot at us. He must have been hiding behind a tree or something.

"We better do as he says," Flip said.

"Listen," Satch said calmly, "I been in plenty of situations like this. That fella don't mean no trouble. He just wants us off his land."

"So what should we do?" I asked.

"Do like I do," Satch said. "Walk slowly to the car. Don't run. That'll only rile him up."

I was shaking, but I followed Satch's lead. Flip and I walked to the wooden fence near Satch's car and climbed it. But just as we got to the top—

Bam!

The gun exploded again, and this time a bullet thwacked against the fence, not more than five feet from my foot.

"Okay, now you can run!" Satch yelled.

The three of us climbed, fell, clawed, or somehow made it over the fence. I didn't need Satch to tell me what to do after that. I was running toward the car like an Olympic sprinter. I even got there before Flip, and he was moving pretty fast.

"You promised me I wouldn't have to run!" Flip shouted.

"Get in the car!" I yelled, diving into the back-seat and slamming the door behind me.

Flip and Satch jumped in the front. Satch turned the key and I was glad the engine started, because there was another gunshot, and I thought I heard the bullet ricochet off the dirt behind the car. Satch hit the gas and the wheels spun a second or two before they finally grabbed the road and we tore out of there.

"Woooo-heeee!" Flip screamed as we pulled away. "Look at us! We're like outlaws! We should call our-selves the Baseball Banditos!"

"That guy shoots worse than I do!" Satch said, cackling with laughter. "But still, sometimes it's best to get outta town fast."

The two of them were slapping each other on the back like they were best buddies or something. I couldn't believe the laughing lunatic in the front seat was the same Flip Valentini who had been worried that traveling through time might be too dangerous.

Me, I was still curled up in a ball on the backseat, just in case that nut with the gun got off another shot. I didn't sit up until we were miles away from that field.

Satch drove for about an hour, then he and Flip switched places to give Satch a rest. I could tell Flip was having the time of his life, driving an old Packard with Satchel Paige sitting next to him. He and Satch started singing old songs Flip remembered from his childhood, and Satch told more of his hard-to-believe baseball stories.

I was anxious to get to Pittsburgh already. We had been in the car for a long time. The sun was dipping low in the sky. I was getting hungry and I had to go to the bathroom.

There was a sign at the side of the road: WELCOME TO VIRGINIA. We came to a little town. There were some African Americans on the street here, I noticed. We passed a gas station and Satch said it would be a good place to stop and fill up. Flip pulled over.

"Hey, check it out, Stosh," Flip said. "Gas is nineteen cents a gallon!"

"Too bad we can't bring some home with us," I said.

A black guy came out of the gas station to pump the gas. He took one look at Satch and pointed at him.

"You're Satchel Paige!" the guy gushed.

"All day," Satch replied.

The attendant looked at Flip and me for a moment, as if he was wondering why two white guys would be riding in the same car with Satchel Paige.

"They're with me," Satch explained, and the guy went to pump the gas.

I hopped out of the car and found the bathroom. I was in there doing my business when a piece of paper taped to the wall caught my eye.

I grabbed the paper and brought it out to the car with me. Flip was looking at a map while Satch paid for the gas. I got in the backseat and showed them the flyer.

"What's up with this?" I asked.

"Green is my favorite color," Satch said. "When somebody waves that green in my face, I can't resist."

We got back on the road and it wasn't long before we pulled into a parking lot next to a ballfield. It was a rickety old dump with wooden bleachers.

"I assume this is *not* the World Series," Flip said as we got out of the car.

"Son, this is about as far from the World Series as you're gonna get," Satch said, grabbing his glove out of the trunk.

We walked over to the ballfield, and the first thing I noticed were the lights. Night games must have been a novelty in the early 1940s, because the lights were really primitive.

There were these giant poles that were mounted on the tops of trucks, and at the top of each pole was a big floodlight pointing down at the field. There was a truck near the first base line, one near the third base line, one behind the plate, and three of them right in the middle of the outfield. If somebody hit a deep fly ball out there, the outfielder could very easily run headfirst into a truck.

Behind the outfield fence, there was this big generator that sounded like an old steam locomotive. It must have provided the power for the lights. When it coughed or sputtered, the bulbs went dim for a moment and then got bright again.

A sign at the gate said that admission was 75 cents. Flip pulled out some of the change Laverne had given him back at the diner, but we didn't need it.

"They're with me," Satch told the guy taking tickets, and he let us in.

As soon as we were inside the gate, a big black guy with a cigar in his mouth came rushing over to Satch.

"You're late, Paige!" he sputtered. "I got three thousand people here demanding their money back!"

"I hit a dog on the road, Bobby," Satch told the guy as he winked at me. "Had to take the poor fella to the animal hospital. The little guy looked like he was fixin' to die. I stayed with him all afternoon and thank the Lord he pulled through. You understand, don't you, Bobby?"

"Don't be runnin' your mouth on me, Paige! I got a business here! No show, no dough!"

"Oh, stop flappin' your gums, Bobby," Satch said. "You'll bust a gasket. Don't worry none. When old Satch shows up late, it makes folks want him even more."

"You almost gave me a heart attack, Paige!" Bobby said before storming off.

The bleachers were full. Most, but not all, of the crowd was black. Satch looked around and nodded his head with satisfaction.

"This Hitler fella sure is good for business," he said. "Ever since Ted Williams and Bobby Feller and Hank Greenberg went away to fight them Nazis, more folks than ever want to see me pitch."

"How come you're not in the service, Satch?" I asked.

"Well, if Uncle Sam don't consider me man enough to sleep in his hotels or eat in his restaurants, he can't very well 'spect me to fight for his democracy, can he?" Satch replied. "Besides, I got flat feet, so they wouldn't take me."

Satch led us through a tunnel behind the stands. A few kids were hanging around waiting for autographs, and Satch signed one for each of them. Just before he reached a door marked LOCKER ROOM, a white guy wearing a jacket and tie stuck a piece of paper and a pen in his face. Satch signed it and handed it back to the guy.

"Ain't you a bit old to be collectin' autographs?" Satch asked him.

"I'm a lawyer, Mr. Paige," the guy said, handing Satch a business card. "I represent your wife. Those are divorce papers you signed."

Satch stopped for a moment and watched as the guy walked away.

"I didn't know you were married, Satch," I said.

"I guess I ain't anymore," he replied.

Satch didn't seem to be all that troubled by what had just happened. He pulled open the door to the locker room and put his other arm on Flip's shoulder.

"This won't take long, boys," he said. "I only gotta pitch two innings. Get yourself some seats and enjoy the show. But don't be pullin' that speed gun of yours out here. I'm savin' up my best stuff to throw at Josh in Pittsburgh."

Satch said he'd meet us later. So Flip and I found some open seats a few rows behind the dugout on the first base side. I talked Flip into using some of our change to buy hot dogs and sodas. They were real cheap, so we still had money left in case of emergency. Flip complained about having to eat junk food, but he bit into that hot dog like it was a gourmet meal.

I looked around. Flip and I were the only white people in our section. It felt a little weird. We were the "minority group." Flip said this must be what it feels like for a lot of African Americans *all* the time.

"Ladies and gentlemen," a voice boomed out of a loudspeaker. "Welcome to Victory Field. You are in for a rare treat because this evening we bring to you the greatest baseball show on earth. The kings of the diamond. Let's hear it for the world-renowned . . . IN . . . DI . . . AN . . . APOLIS . . . CLOWNS!"

The crowd applauded and the Clowns took the field.

Now, I need to explain something here. In the major leagues, the Detroit Tigers aren't really tigers. The St. Louis Cardinals and the Baltimore Orioles aren't really birds. But the Indianapolis Clowns were real, honest-to-goodness clowns!

"Well, *this* is different," Flip said.

The third baseman had white makeup and war paint on his face, and he was wearing a grass skirt over his uniform. The second baseman wore a tuxedo and a top hat. He balanced a baseball on his hat and tilted his head to make the ball roll around and around the brim. The first baseman had on a regular uniform, but he was wearing a glove that was about four feet tall. The shortstop was a midget who had the words "Shorty Potato" on his back.

One outfielder had a really long beard and he

was dressed like a woman. Another was dressed like a fireman. The third wore a polka-dotted clown costume and walked on his hands all the way from the dugout to centerfield.

The pitcher was dressed like an Egyptian pharaoh, with KING TUT written on his back. The catcher dragged out a rocking chair, which he put behind home plate and sat in while he warmed up the pitcher.

Except for the catcher and pitcher, all the other players were dancing to the big-band music that was coming out of the speakers. The guy in the tux was juggling three baseballs.

"Well, *this* is different," Flip said, biting into his hot dog.

We watched the infielders throwing a ball around, or at least I *thought* they were throwing a ball around. When I looked more closely, I could see that they were just *pretending* to throw a ball around. They were doing a baseball pantomime show, scooping up imaginary grounders, throwing invisible balls, and making spectacular fake diving catches in slow motion. The whole thing was like a circus, and the crowd loved it.

"Leading off for the New York Stars," boomed the announcer, "Jimmy Mitchell."

The batter came out of the other dugout, and all the clowning suddenly stopped. King Tut went into his windup and threw the first pitch.

"Steeerike one!" shouted the umpire.

The batter took a couple of balls, and then hit a grounder to third. The third baseman—the guy with the grass skirt—expertly scooped up the ball and threw it to first . . . from behind his back! The first baseman was lying on the ground with his leg up in the air and the glove stuck on the end of his foot. He caught the ball that way! It was the most amazing thing I had ever seen.

These guys were clowns, but they could really play.

"Ladies and gentleman," boomed the announcer, "coaching at first base is Bullet Billy Roberts, who set a Negro League record for pitching two games at the same time—his first and his last."

King Tut struck the next guy out. Before the batter went back to the dugout, King Tut ran off the mound, grabbed the guy's bat, and pretended to give him some hitting pointers. The crowd roared. The next guy popped up to short, where the midget shortstop tossed away his glove and caught the ball in his baggy pants.

Three outs. The Clowns ran, skipped, hopped, juggled, and cartwheeled their way back to their dugout.

Before the New York Stars took the field, some acrobats who called themselves the Flying Nesbit Family put on a little show in the infield. It was amazing. Then the Stars came out. They looked perfectly normal, especially after seeing the Clowns.

The Stars threw real baseballs around to warm up. But one of the Stars was missing. There was

announcer told the crowd, "Satchel guarantees he will strike out the first six batters, or every fan will receive free admission tomorrow."

A few people cheered, but one guy got up and shouted, "There ain't no game tomorrow!" The crowd cracked up.

Satch swung his right arm around a few times and lobbed four pitches to the catcher to warm up. That seemed enough. He held up a hand to quiet down the crowd as the batter walked to the plate.

"No need to tote that wood up here, son," he yelled to the batter. "You ain't gonna need it. You'll be sittin' your butt back on that bench before you can work up a sweat."

The crowd laughed. The batter pumped his bat back and forth menacingly.

"Which pitch do you want, son?" Satch asked. "I call my fastball the Midnight Rider. But I'll give you my Bat Dodger, Jump Ball, or Whipsey-Dipsey-Do, if you'd prefer."

"Just throw the ball, old man," the batter shouted back.

"Okey-dokey."

Satch windmilled the ball around slowly one, two, three, then four times. He kicked his leg way up high over his head and held it there so everybody in the stands could see the sole of his shoe, where the word "Fastball" was written in white letters. He came forward until his foot hit the ground. Somehow, impossibly, he didn't release the ball until a split second later.

Satch had a funny windup.

The ball shot out of his hand like a bullet. The batter was totally fooled by Satch's motion and swung late. It seemed impossible for someone to wind up so slowly and then throw a ball so hard. The ball popped into the catcher's mitt.

"Steeeeerike one!" shouted the ump.

"Oh, you shoulda chose," Satch said. "That was my Hesitation Pitch."

"He can't do that!" the batter yelled at the ump. "That's an illegal pitch!"

"Get back in the batter's box," said the ump.

"What do you wanna swing and miss at now?" Satch asked the batter. "You want my Wobbly Ball, Little Tom, or my Four-Day Creeper?"

The batter didn't answer, so Satch went into his funny windup and whipped one in, sidearm this time. No swing.

"Steeerike two!" shouted the ump.

"I call that my Bee Ball," Satch informed the crowd. "'Cause it *be* right where I want it to be."

The batter had two strikes on him now, and he looked really determined. Satch didn't ask him which pitch he wanted this time. He just wound up like usual. But instead of throwing the ball hard, he lofted a high lob way up in the air.

The ball rose maybe thirty feet and hung up there for what seemed like an hour. The batter looked like he wanted to kill the thing. When the ball finally came down, he swung so hard that he spun around and fell down.

"Steeeerike threeeeeeee!" yelled the ump. "Yer out!"

The crowd went nuts.

"That was my Nothin' Ball," Satch said after the fans had calmed down. "'Cause it don't do nothin'."

The Clown in the grass skirt was swinging a big war club in the on-deck circle. He dropped it and picked up a regular bat before coming to the plate.

Satch threw him a fastball, and he couldn't come close to catching up with it.

"Whatsa matter?" Satch asked. "Too hot for ya?"

The guy got ready again, and Satch blew another one right by him.

"Got a headache yet?" Satch asked. "'Cause I'm throwin' aspirins, and you're gonna need 'em."

The Clown got set again, and Satch gave him nothing but heat for strike three.

"That hummer just sang a sweet song!" Satch shouted. "The finest music I ever heard."

Two outs. The next Clown came up and Satch fanned him in similar fashion with three fastballs— one overhand, one sidearm, and one underhand.

The crowd erupted in cheers as Satch ambled slowly back into the dugout.

After one inning, there was no score. While the Stars jogged back to their dugout, a jeep came tearing out across the outfield with one of the Clowns driving it. He had that gigantic glove on his hand. One of the other Clowns picked up a bat and started whacking fungoes to the outfield. The Clown driving the jeep circled around, trying to catch the balls in his big glove. He missed the first four, but when he caught the fifth one the crowd gave him a standing ovation.

The Clowns put on a great show between innings, and they clearly knew how to play the game. But I wasn't sure that the game they were playing was baseball. One guy slid into second about five feet short, and he pretended to *swim* the rest of the way to the base. The whole thing looked sort of humiliating to tell you the truth, and I asked Flip what he thought.

"You gotta remember, these guys are banned from pro ball," Flip said. "They're tryin' to make a living. They're tryin' to entertain folks any way they can. Make 'em forget about the war goin' on over in Europe for a while."

As Flip was talking, I noticed a white girl making her way down our row. When she got closer to us, I recognized her. It was Laverne, that cute waitress we met back at the diner! She had a suitcase with her.

"Remember me?" she said, flinging an arm around Flip like they were boyfriend and girlfriend.

Remember her? How could anyone forget her? With that little pink hat on her head, she looked even prettier than before.

"What are *you* doing here?" Flip asked.

Flip could be such a dope! Here was this beautiful girl throwing herself at him, and he was acting like she shouldn't be there. If it was me, I would have hugged and kissed her and asked her what she was doing for dinner that night.

"I ran away from home," Laverne said.

"What?!"

"You saw what my daddy was like. I couldn't take it anymore. Tomorrow I'll be eighteen years old, and I can do what I want."

"How did you end up here?" Flip asked.

"I was hitching a ride to Pittsburgh when I saw

this poster about Satchel Paige playing against the Clowns. I thought I'd find you here. And I was right."

She gave Flip a peck on the cheek.

"Remember me?" I said. "Joe Stoshack? Stosh?"

"Oh, yeah. Hi," she said, totally unimpressed. I bet she would have liked me more if I had big muscles like Flip. And if I was five years older.

The Indianapolis Clowns were back on the field again. We got Laverne a hot dog and Flip explained the fine points of Clown baseball to her. The third baseman was now sitting on a lawn chair next to third base and reading a newspaper. Somebody hit a pop-up at him, and he stuck out his glove and caught it without looking away from the paper. Laverne thought that was the funniest thing she'd ever seen. She had a nice laugh.

The Stars went down in order and Satch took the mound again. The leadoff batter for the Clowns was that bearded guy who was dressed up like a woman. Laverne couldn't stop giggling.

"You're an overrated bum, Paige!" the guy yelled. "You should be in an old-age home!"

Satch just laughed. He reared back and threw a fastball high and tight. The guy dove out of the way and landed face-first in the dirt.

"Oooooooh!" went the crowd.

"Take your base," called the umpire.

"What?!" Satch complained. "The pitch didn't hit 'im!"

"It hit his beard," said the ump.

"Those whiskers can't rightly be called no part of

a man," Satch yelled. "They is air!"

"Take your base."

The guy brushed the dirt off his skirt and jogged to first. The fans started yelling. Getting on base against Satchel Paige was big news. Satch stomped around the mound a while before facing the next batter, Shorty Potato, the midget shortstop. The guy must have been about the size of a fire hydrant, and his strike zone was a few inches at most. Satch had great control, but he couldn't pitch to Shorty Potato. He walked on four pitches.

Runners on first and second. Nobody out. People were screaming for a hit.

Satch wasn't fooling around anymore. The guy wearing the tuxedo was up, and Satch threw him smoke. The guy squared around and dropped a perfect bunt down the third baseline. The Stars third baseman ran in and tried to barehand it, but the ball slipped out of his fingers.

Everybody was safe. Bases loaded. Nobody out. Satch was in a jam. The crowd was going crazy now.

Satch asked the umpire for time-out, and he leaned over and put his hands on his knees like he was going to throw up or something. A hush fell over the crowd.

A pretty girl wearing a nurse's uniform came running out of the Stars' dugout. She was holding one of those black bags doctors always carry.

"Whatsa matter, Satch?" the nurse asked, loud enough for everyone to hear.

"Must be nerves, ma'am," Satch said, rubbing his

belly. "I got the miseries playing in my stomach. I might have to go home."

"No!" the fans hollered.

"You got yourself into this mess, Paige!" some fan yelled. "Let's see you get out of it!"

The nurse reached into her bag and pulled out a spoon and some medicine. She filled the spoon and stuck it in Satch's mouth. Satch stood there for about a minute. Then he let out a belch that we could hear in the bleachers. Everybody laughed.

"Okay," he announced. "My stomach is peaceable now."

Everybody whistled when the nurse ran off the field. The hitter stepped into the batter's box. Satch turned to face his outfielders and waved his arms, signaling that they should move in. The three of them took a few steps forward, and he waved to them again. They took a few more steps toward the infield, but Satch kept waving them in, more urgently.

"*All* the way in," he hollered. "You boys can have the rest of this inning off. I'll take it from here."

"He's pullin' the outfield!" Flip marveled. The crowd gasped when all three outfielders jogged off the field.

The batter grinned as he took a few practice swings. All he needed to do was hit a ball past the infield and the Clowns would score three runs. Maybe four.

Next, Satch turned toward his infielders.

"You too," he shouted, waving them off the field. "You boys look like you need a rest."

The first baseman, second baseman, third baseman, and shortstop jogged to the dugout. The only Stars left on the field were Satch and his catcher. The crowd was buzzing. People around us started pulling out money and betting on whether or not Satch would strike the batter out.

"Is he crazy?" asked Laverne.

"Maybe," Flip said. "Maybe not."

14

A New Pitcher

I HAD NEVER HEARD OF A PITCHER CALLING IN HIS fielders and working with no defense behind him. It was insane! Without any fielders to hold them on, the runners at first, second, and third took good long leads. The field looked so empty out there.

"Now it's just you and me, son," Satch said to the batter. "Ain't this cozy?"

"Let's see what you got," the batter shouted back, licking his lips. All he had to do was put the ball in play and the Clowns would score four runs.

Satch windmilled the ball over his head a few times and burned the first pitch in. The batter looked at it.

"Steeeeerike one!" called the ump, and the crowd's noise went up a notch.

The batter got set again and Satch gave him another fastball. Swing and a miss.

"Steeeeerike two!" called the ump.

The fans were screaming now. Satch stepped off the mound and wiped his forehead with his sleeve. The batter dug his cleats into the batter's box. Satch went into his windup and the guy took a furious swing. The only thing he hit was air.

"Steeeeerike three!"

The crowd roared as the next Clown—their catcher—stepped in to face Satch. One out.

"He should bunt it down the first or third baseline," I said to Flip and Laverne. "Satch wouldn't have a chance to field the ball."

"Oh, that wouldn't be any fun," Flip said.

Satch was throwing all fastballs, so he didn't even bother looking for a sign. He got two quick strikes on the batter, who called time and stepped out of the batter's box for a moment.

"Whatsa matter?" Satch asked. "You nervous? Hey, *I'm* the one that ain't got no defense!"

The crowd laughter turned to cheers when Satch hummed in another fast one and the guy waved at it.

"Steeeeerike three!" yelled the ump. "Two outs!"

The next Clown up must have been reading my mind, because as soon as Satch wound up, the batter squared around to bunt. Satch threw the ball way inside, and the Clown dove backward like a train was coming at him.

"Don't be buntin' on me!" Satch yelled as the batter got up off the dirt. "Take your three swings like a man!"

That's exactly what the guy did.

Strike one.

Strike two.

Strike three.

And that was it. Satch had struck out the side with the bases loaded and the only fielder in fair territory was himself. The crowd just about exploded as Satch walked off the mound. I thought the wooden stands were going to collapse. Flip was going crazy. Laverne stuck two fingers in her mouth and let out an ear-splitting whistle.

After that second inning, the Stars replaced Satch with another pitcher. He wasn't nearly as much fun to watch, but we stuck around anyway. We really didn't have a choice, because Satch was our ride. I figured he'd come get us when he was ready to go.

I kept looking over at Flip and Laverne to see how they were getting along. They were talking to each other, but it didn't look like any romantic sparks were flying. I kept whispering in Flip's ear that he should put his arm around her, but he wouldn't do it.

The score was 2-2 in the eighth inning when the manager of the Clowns came out on the field carrying a bullhorn.

"Attention, ladies and gentlemen," he called. "Due to illness, our pitching staff is deeply depleted. We got nobody left."

"Boooooooooo!" the crowd replied.

"But I have good news!" the manager hollered. "I'm lookin' for a fresh arm. Anybody out there know how to pitch?"

A buzz went through the crowd, but nobody came out of the stands.

"Stosh told me you're a ballplayer, Flip," Laverne said. "Why don't you go out there and pitch?"

"I'm really not that good," Flip mumbled.

"Go on, Flip!" I said. "What've you got to lose?"

"Nah, it's been years since I threw a ball."

Flip was hopeless. I couldn't take it anymore. I got up out of my seat.

"Hey," I shouted, "my friend here can pitch!"

"Stosh!" Flip whispered. "I'm not goin' out there!"

"What's your friend's name, son?" the manager asked.

"His name is Flip," I said, even as Flip was trying to put his hand over my mouth. "Flip Valentini. He's a great pitcher."

"We got a white boy here who's a great pitcher!" the manager hollered. "Come on down, Flip!"

"Go ahead, Flip," urged Laverne. "Show 'em what you can do."

The fans started stamping their feet on the bleachers and chanting, "Flip! Flip! Flip!"

I don't think I ever saw anyone look so embarrassed in my life. Reluctantly, Flip stood up, and everyone cheered. People clapped him on the back as he made his way down to the front row. He climbed over the low fence next to the dugout.

Somebody gave Flip a glove, a hat, and a pair of cleats to put on. The manager gave him a little shove and Flip walked out to the pitcher's mound.

"Now pitching for the Indianapolis Clowns," said the announcer, "FLIP VAL . . . EN . . . TI . . . NI!"

The catcher tossed him a ball, and Flip promptly threw his first warm-up pitch over the catcher's head and against the backstop. A few hecklers shouted out good-natured insults. Flip looked nervous, but settled down and found the plate with his next pitch.

You could tell Flip was a natural pitcher. He had a nice, easy motion. The ball popped into the catcher's mitt like it had some velocity. It was obvious that he knew what he was doing out there.

"I'm so excited!" Laverne squealed, crossing her fingers.

"Batter up!" called the ump.

Laverne and I leaned forward in our seats. *This is perfect*, I thought. Even if Flip didn't know how to get to first base with Laverne, she'd be so impressed by his pitching that she'd fall even more crazy in love with him. Girls dig jocks.

"Flip! Flip! Flip!" chanted the crowd.

On the mound, Flip got set and the Star first baseman stepped up to the plate. He was a big, mean-looking guy. Flip went into his windup. He threw. The guy swung.

Bam!

I don't think I ever saw a ball go so far. It was

still rising when it cleared the left field fence. It probably landed somewhere near Pittsburgh.

"Oooooooooh!" groaned the crowd.

"Nice changeup, whitey!" somebody yelled. "Now let's see your fastball!"

"That was a lucky hit, Flip!" I hollered as the batter trotted around the bases.

"You can do it, Flip!" Laverne shouted.

The ump tossed Flip another ball. The next batter came up to the plate. Flip took a deep breath, kicked up his leg, and tried again.

Bam!

Another rocket. This one went to right field, slamming against the scoreboard so hard, I think it made a dent. Back-to-back homers. Ouch.

"Don't get discouraged, Flip!" I yelled. Flip was walking around the mound, wiping his face with his sleeve.

"You better start working on a knuckleball!" somebody hollered from the crowd.

"Strike this guy out!" shouted Laverne.

The ump tossed Flip another baseball and the next Star came out of the dugout. It was their first baseman. Flip closed his eyes for a moment to compose himself, and then he reared back and buzzed one in.

Bam!

The manager was out of the Clowns' dugout before the ball sailed over the centerfield fence. I couldn't hear what he was saying to Flip on the mound, but I'm pretty sure he wasn't telling him what a great job he had done.

As Flip was leaving the field, the midget short-stop went to the mound.

"Now pitching for the Clowns," boomed the announcer, "SHORTY PO . . . TA . . . TO!"

The crowd had a good laugh at that. When he got to the dugout, Flip threw the glove and the cap against the fence, kicked off the cleats and put on his shoes. Then he marched right off the field and headed for the exit.

"Come on!" I said, grabbing Laverne's hand.

We ran out of our seats and out of the ballpark. After looking around for a few minutes, we found Flip wandering aimlessly around the parking lot. He was cursing to himself, and his face was all flushed, like he had been crying.

"Where are you going?" I asked him.

"I don't know," Flip said disgustedly. "Out of here. Anywhere."

Laverne put her arms around Flip and held him. It seemed to calm him down a little.

"You are *good*, Flip," she whispered in his ear. "You just had a bad day, that's all. Next time, you'll strike those boys out. Mark my words you will. You're gonna be a *great* pitcher someday."

And then she kissed him! I mean, it was a real kiss, on the mouth, just like in the movies!

Man, I wished she was hugging and kissing *me*. Too bad I didn't go out there and let them hit three homers in a row. Girls must dig jocks even more when they mess up and cry.

Suddenly, I got an idea.

"Hey, why don't you come with us?" I asked Laverne. "We're going to see the Negro League World Series in Pittsburgh with Satchel Paige. I bet Satch wouldn't mind another passenger."

"You think?" she asked, her arms still around Flip.

"Sure don't mind one as pretty as this young lady," somebody said.

We all turned around. It was Satch. He was back in his street clothes and he had a wad of ten-dollar bills in his hand.

"The game's not over yet," Flip said. "How come you left, Satch?"

"I done my part and I got paid," he said. "Let's get outta here."

"Not so fast!" someone behind us said. We all wheeled around.

"Daddy!" cried Laverne.

15

The World Series

LAVERNE'S FATHER WAS STANDING THERE NOT MORE than twenty feet away. Man, he looked like he was going to kill all of us.

Flip took his hands off Laverne like she was a hot stove and backed two quick steps away from her.

"Get in the car, Laverne!" her father said.

"I'm eighteen years old, Daddy, and I—," she started.

"Not yet you ain't!" he said. "Come with me right now, young lady!"

Laverne looked at Flip, like he was supposed to do something.

"You should go with your father," Flip said softly. "It's the right thing to do."

"But I want to be with *you*," Laverne said. "See, Daddy? I told you how nice he is. Flip is sensitive and mature. Not like other boys."

"Let's *go*, Laverne!" her father snapped.

She reached out for Flip's hand, but her father slapped it away. He stuck his face near Flip's and warned, "You so much as *touch* my daughter and you're a dead man. You got that, son?"

"Yes, sir."

He shot a dirty look at Satch for good measure, grabbed Laverne's hand and led her to his car. She turned around to look at Flip one more time before she got inside. I could see her sobbing in the backseat as the car pulled away.

There wasn't anything else we could do. Satch, Flip, and I got into Satch's car. We still had a long ride to Pittsburgh, and Satch seemed to be in a bigger hurry now. Flip looked out the window as we accelerated out of the parking lot.

"That girl is in love with you, Flip!" I said after a few miles passed. "She ran away from home to be with you. I can't believe you let her get away."

"It was the right thing to do," Flip said quietly.

"Why do you always have to do the right thing?" I asked. "How about doing what's right for *you* once in a while?"

Nobody said anything for a few minutes. Satch finally broke the silence.

"You got a thing or two to learn about women," he said to Flip, "and you got a thing or two to learn about pitchin' too."

"You got that right," Flip sighed.

"So which do you wanna learn first?"

"Women?" I suggested.

"The two strongest things in the world are money and women," Satch said. "The things you do for women you wouldn't do for anything else. Same with money. But you got to be mighty careful of love. Gettin' married is like walkin' in front of a firing squad. But you don't give up women no more than a carp gives up dough balls."

"I'm shy around girls," Flip said.

"Ain't nothin' wrong with bein' shy," replied Satch. "That girl was all big eyes for you. So that shy thing is workin' and you should stick with it. But you got to close the deal, man. If you want somethin', you got to go *get* it. That goes for women, for baseball, for any-thing. 'Cause nine times outta ten, you let somethin' like that slip away, and it's gone. No second chances."

Satch went on for a while, and at some point I noticed he wasn't telling Flip how to deal with women anymore. He was telling Flip how to deal with hitters.

"A bullfighter can tell what a bull is gonna do by watchin' his knees," Satch said. "A pitcher can do the same thing. You see the batter's knees move, and you can tell just what his weaknesses are. I was watchin' you warm up. You got good stuff. *Real* good stuff. But you need work on your motion and your control. You just gotta let the ball flow out of your hand like it's water. And slow down. Too many pitch-ers got the hurry-ups."

"That's it?" Flip asked.

"Pitchin' is easy," Satch said. "It's women that are hard. Just throw the ball where you want it to go. Home plate don't move. Keep the ball away from the bat and you'll be fine. And never throw two fast-balls the same speed."

"Thanks, Satch."

"Don't mention it. You go where learnin' is flyin' 'round, some of it's bound to light on you."

The road was straight and smooth, and Satch wasn't afraid to step on the gas. The needle was over 70 miles per hour, and we passed a sign that said WELCOME TO WEST VIRGINIA. Satch and Flip were talking baseball, but I must have dozed off, because suddenly I was jolted awake by the sound of a siren.

Satch cursed and pulled over to the side of the road. A police car stopped behind us.

"Don't go shootin' off your mouths," Satch told us as he rolled down the window. "Let me do the talkin'."

The policeman got out of his car and walked slowly up to the window. He looked the car up and down and checked us out.

"Nice automobile you have here, for a colored boy," he said.

"Thank you, officer," Satch said.

"It yours?" the cop said. "You didn't steal it from nobody, did you?"

"No, sir," Satch said. "Got my ownership papers right here."

The cop looked over the papers carefully. I kept expecting him to recognize Satch's name and suddenly get all nice and ask him for an autograph or something. But he never did.

"This is Satchel Paige, officer," I said, leaning forward. "He's famous!"

The cop looked up and glared at me.

"Son, did this colored fellow kidnap you?"

"No, of course not," I said.

"Then shut your mouth."

"Officer," Satch said politely, "I'm sorry I was speedin'. But we're in a rush to get to Pittsburgh."

"Boy, you drive like you're in a rush to get to heaven," the cop said, handing Satch a ticket. "It's gonna cost you forty dollars. I reckon that's a whole lot of money to you."

Satch pulled out his wallet and counted out a bunch of ten-dollar bills.

"I'm gonna give you *eighty* dollars," Satch told the cop, handing over the money, "'cause I'm comin' back this way again tomorrow."

Satch hit the gas and we peeled out of there while the cop was still counting the bills.

"Man," Satch said, "I got so many speeding tickets, the police should give me a discount."

We drove past a sign saying we had entered Pennsylvania, and it wasn't long before the flat countryside turned into houses, factories, smokestacks, and lots of signs with the word "Pittsburgh" in them. Satch knew his way around the city streets. Soon we were outside a ballpark. I saw those big letters: FORBES FIELD.

"Isn't this where the Pittsburgh Pirates used to play?" I asked as Satch pulled into the parking lot.

"Still do," Satch replied. "They rent it out to us when they're on the road."

Black people were not allowed to use the locker room, Satch explained as he pulled a brown-and-white Kansas City Monarchs uniform out of the trunk of his car. He put it on right in the parking lot. The cap had a "KC" on it and the Monarchs logo was a baseball with a crown on top.

As we crossed the street to the ballpark, Flip leaned over and told me that Forbes Field doesn't exist anymore in our time, and that Babe Ruth hit his last home run there.

A newsboy was selling papers on the corner, and Flip said he wanted to see what they had to say about the World Series. He picked a newspaper up off the pile.

"You ain't gonna find nothin' 'bout *our* World Series in there," Satch said. "Better get a colored paper."

Man, *everything* was segregated. Blacks and whites not only had their own water fountains, hotels, restaurants, and baseball leagues, they even had their own newspapers. It was like there were two separate worlds living side by side.

Satch picked up a copy of something called *The Pittsburgh Courier* and Flip tossed the newsboy a nickel. There was an article about the World Series right on the front page.

Grays, Kansas

AMERICAN, NATIONAL LOOP LEADERS PLAY IN WORLD SERIES

PITTSBURGH, PA, Sept. 9 — Thirty-two thousand baseball fans may test the capacity of Forbes Field on Thursday, when the mighty Monarchs of Kansas City and the Homestead Grays cross bats and lock horns here in Smoketown.

The Monarchs, with the great "Satchel" Paige, and the Grays, led by power-hitting Josh Gibson, again have dominated their respective leagues, the Negro American and the Negro National, and will launch the series to determine the real kings of the sepia diamond.

Lanky Leroy, the ace of the Monarchs' hurling staff, who is rated one of the greatest pitchers of all time, will have vengeance in his heart plus blazing speed and baffling curves in his million dollar arm as he steps to the rubber to face the National Leaguers. Josh Gibson, slugger extraordinaire, is equally determined to get the better of the matchup. The series promises to be a showdown of unprecedented proportions. Tickets for the game will be on sale at Forbes Field.

Bucks Take Two

Once Satch got us inside the ballpark, it sure looked like the World Series. There was a brass band playing in the centerfield stands. People were hawking scorecards and souvenirs. The place was jammed with fans. Most of them were black, and most were all dressed up like they were going to church. The smell of hot roasted peanuts made me hungry.

"Tell me again what Josh said 'bout me?" Satch asked us.

"He said he's gonna shut your big mouth in Pittsburgh," I answered.

"We'll see 'bout that."

People recognized Satch immediately. As he led us down toward the field, little kids ran over to him. They didn't want autographs. They just wanted to *touch* him. Once they made contact with him, they would just stand there staring at their hands in disbelief, saying things like, "I touched him!" or "I'll never wash this hand again!"

We finally made it down to the front row, near the third base dugout. Satch handed Flip two tickets and told us to enjoy the game. He'd meet us at the front entrance when it was over.

"Make sure you check my speed when I'm pitchin' to Josh," he instructed us. "I'll be throwin' my hardest."

As soon as he hopped over the low fence onto the field, a guy wearing a Monarch uniform charged over to him.

"You're late, Satchel!" the guy said, all agitated. "You missed the team warm-up."

"Calm yourself, Frank," Satch said. "You'll live longer. Only warm-up I need is to shake hands with the catcher."

Flip and I bought two bags of roasted peanuts from a vendor and sat down. One of the Homestead Grays was taking batting practice, and the rest were warming up on the first and third base sides. Their uniforms had a large "GR" on one side of the chest and "AYS" on the other side.

We spotted Josh Gibson, Cool Papa Bell, and a few of the other players we had met on the bus. They waved hello as they played catch in front of us. Josh's son, the kid we had seen back in the diner, was the Grays' batboy.

Photographers were snapping pictures, and one of them had a good idea. He pulled Satch out of the Monarchs' dugout and brought him over to Josh Gibson so they could pose together.

"Five bucks says I strike you out today."

Josh and Satch were only about ten feet in front of us, and we could hear every word they said.

"Dogface!" Satch said, shaking Josh's hand. "How you doin'? Five bucks says I strike you out today."

"You got a bet, Satch," Josh replied.

"Gibson, your turn for batting practice," somebody shouted.

Josh jogged over to the Grays' dugout and came out with the longest bat I had ever seen. A hush fell over the crowd as he stepped into the batting cage. The peanut vendors stopped selling their peanuts. The brass band stopped playing their instruments. Everyone who was doing anything stopped to watch.

The batting practice pitcher waited until Josh was ready. Josh rolled up his sleeve and spread his legs wide apart. He gripped the bat at the very end and held it up high. He didn't dig and scratch at the dirt, and he didn't wag his bat around the way a lot of hitters do. He looked like a statue. The only movement I could see was in Josh's mouth. He curled his tongue like a hot dog. Then he nodded that he was ready.

The batting practice pitcher wound up and threw. Josh didn't bend his back or knees, and he didn't take a big stride forward. He stood flat footed. He waited until the ball was almost on him. Then he lifted his left foot up very slightly and at the last possible instant attacked the ball with his arms and wrists.

A hush fell over the crowd.

It was a quick, fluid, compact stroke, a classic swing. It almost seemed like he took the ball out of the catcher's mitt.

There was a distinct *crack* when Josh's bat made contact with the ball. It was a crack I had only heard once before, when I went back to 1932 to see

Babe Ruth's famous "called shot" home run. The sound that Ruth's bat made hitting a ball was the same sound that Josh's bat made. I'll never forget that sound.

The ball whistled out of the batting cage on a low trajectory, barely over the pitcher's head. But the spin on it must have been tremendous, because then the ball hopped up and soared like a golf ball. It was over the centerfield fence almost before you could snap your fingers.

"Oooooooh!" moaned the crowd.

"Maybe he *will* shut Satch's mouth," Flip said.

Josh pounded about a dozen balls over the fence, one after the other. Then he signaled to the pitcher that he was done, as if he wanted to save some of those long balls for when they would count.

"You're gonna break that bat, Josh," one of the Grays said.

"I don't break bats," he replied before going to the dugout. "I wear 'em out."

The players cleared the field. Satch grabbed his glove and was getting ready to pitch the first inning when his manager called him back to the dugout.

"You ain't startin', Paige," he said.

"What?!"

"You showed up late. So you sit."

Satch threw his glove down and sulked in the dugout. The announcer introduced the Monarchs as they ran out on the field. A guy named Hilton Smith was their starting pitcher.

He was good too. Smith retired the Grays in order in the first inning. Josh Gibson didn't get the chance to hit, because he was fourth in the batting order.

When the Grays took the field, Josh came out with his catching gear on. Buck O'Neil led off for the Monarchs. When O'Neil stepped up to the plate, Josh started in trash-talking loud enough for the first few rows to hear.

"So this is the famous Mr. Buck O'Neil," Josh said. "I been readin' a lot 'bout you in the papers. You didn't do too good last Friday, did you? Well, you're gonna do worse today."

"Oh, hush your mouth, Josh," O'Neil said.

The pitcher, Roy Partlow, pumped in strike one.

"Oh, you missed that one," Josh said. "Too bad. Now, Mr. Buck, here comes one right down the middle. See if you can hit it."

Buck O'Neil took a big swing and fouled the ball off to the right. Strike two.

"What? Only a foul?" Josh said. "Okay. Don't go swinging at the next one, 'cause we're gonna waste it outside."

The pitch came in and O'Neil leaned over the plate to foul it off.

"Oops!" Josh said. "Sorry. My pitcher messed up and hit the corner. Let's do that one over."

This time the pitch was way outside, but Buck O'Neil took a wild cut at it anyway and missed everything.

"That would be three strikes, Mr. Buck," Josh said

as the umpire called O'Neil out. "You are excused for the time being. Perhaps you'll do better next time."

It went on like that. Loud, fast, exciting baseball. The players didn't hide their emotions, the way they seem to in major league games. When a guy struck out, he got mad, and he showed it. The players took more chances, running the bases recklessly and diving for any ball within reach. The fans really got into the game too, heckling or shouting funny remarks as the mood struck them.

Hilton Smith breezed through the first eight innings. Josh didn't get a hit and the Grays couldn't score on Smith. It looked like he might pitch the whole game, and Satch would never even get the chance to face Josh.

But the Monarchs had a 2-0 lead going into the ninth when an announcement came over the public address system.

"Coming in to pitch for Kansas City, LEROY . . . SATCHEL . . . PAIGE!"

16

Satch versus Josh

EVEN BEFORE SATCH PUT A FOOT ON THE FIELD, THE crowd was roaring. Some of the fans loved him, and some hated him. With every slow-motion step he took toward the mound, the noise level rose. It didn't quiet down until the batter, Boojum Wilson, stepped up to the plate. Satch got set to pitch the ninth inning with a two-run lead.

"Ain't no need for signs," he yelled to his catcher. "Just show me the glove and hold it still. I'll hit it."

Satch struck out Boojum Wilson, and the next batter, Jelly Jackson, grounded out to short. It didn't look like we'd have the chance to clock Satch's fastball against Josh. A few fans started making their way toward the exits. I guess they figured a two-run lead was safe with Satch on the mound, and they wanted to beat the traffic out of the parking lot.

I noticed Satch kept looking into the Grays'

dugout. He was looking at Josh. There were two outs now, and Josh wasn't due up for three more batters. It wasn't likely that he was going to get another chance to hit.

"When do I get my five bucks, Satch?" Josh shouted out to the mound.

The next batter, Jerry Benjamin, didn't look intimidated by Satch. He took a strike and a ball, and then lined a single to left. The tying run was at the plate now, with two outs. A guy named Howard Easterling was announced, and he stepped up to the plate.

Satch looked at Josh in the dugout again, and then he called time-out. He motioned for first base-man Buck O'Neil to come over to the mound. The two of them looked like they were arguing about something. O'Neil called for the manager, Frank Duncan, to come out to the mound.

The crowd was starting to buzz now as the three men seemed to be having a heated discussion. The catcher came out to join the chat too.

"What's going on?" I asked Flip.

"I guess they're talkin' about how they're gonna pitch to Easterling," he replied.

O'Neil finally went back to first base, the catcher went back behind the plate, and Duncan went back to the dugout. Satch got set to pitch. Easterling pumped his bat back and forth.

Then the catcher stuck his glove all the way out to the left. I knew that signal. It meant they were going to walk Easterling intentionally. Satch threw ball one all the way off the plate.

"Why is he walking Easterling?" I asked Flip.

"Beats me," he replied. "That puts the tyin' run on first. Nobody does that."

Satch kept looking in the dugout for Josh.

After taking four balls way off the plate, Easterling trotted to first. Runners on first and second. Still two outs. Buck Leonard came up to hit.

As soon as Leonard settled into the batter's box, the catcher stuck his left arm out again to signal *another* intentional walk!

A buzz swirled around the ballpark as Josh Gibson came out to the on-deck circle, and we all realized what Satch was up to. He was walking those two batters so he could pitch to Josh with the bases loaded!

You just don't *do* that! You don't put two guys into scoring position and give the best hitter in baseball the chance to drive them in and win the game! It's just not *done*. Especially in the World Series!

"He's crazy!" Flip said as Leonard watched ball four go by.

Leonard jogged to first. Bases loaded. Two outs. Ninth inning. 2–0 game. The tying run was on second, the winning run on first. Josh had a little smile on his face as he walked up to the plate. Everybody in the bleachers edged forward.

"Hey," I told Flip. "Get out the radar gun! Satch is gonna give Josh all he's got."

Flip pulled out the radar gun, putting his coat over the top of it so the fans around us wouldn't get suspicious.

"Hey, Josh!" Satch hollered as Josh got into the batter's box. "I hear you're gonna shut my mouth!"

"That's right, Satchel!"

Josh stepped up to the plate with the bases loaded.

Flip pointed the gun toward the mound and fiddled with the buttons on it.

"Josh," Satch called, "remember when you and me were on the Crawfords and you said you were the best hitter in the world and I said I was the best pitcher?"

"I sure do."

"And I said one day we'd face off against each

other in a big game with the bases loaded?"

"Yeah, Satchel. I remember that."

"Well, it looks like today's the day," Satch said.

Flip was still fooling with the gun when Josh took his stance.

"What's the matter?" I asked Flip.

"Something's wrong," he replied. "The thing won't turn on!"

"Maybe the batteries are dead," I said.

"They're new batteries!" Flip replied, hitting the gun with the side of his hand.

Flip was working frantically on the gun. The runners took their leads at first, second, and third base.

"Now listen, Josh," Satch hollered. "I'm not gonna trick you. I'm gonna throw you a fastball letter high. You better swing, 'cause the ump's just gonna call it a strike anyways if you don't."

"Show me what you got," Josh yelled back.

"This thing is busted!" Flip said. "The coach is gonna kill me!"

"You gotta make it work!" I yelled at Flip.

Satch went into his windup and threw a fastball that hissed on its way to the plate. It was probably the fastest pitch I'd ever seen. Josh took a good rip at it and fouled it off to the left side. Strike one. The crowd roared.

Disgusted, Flip put the radar gun away.

"Look at you," Satch yelled at Josh. "You ain't ready up there."

"I'm ready," Josh replied. "Throw it."

"Now look out, Josh, 'cause I'm gonna throw you one a little faster and belt high. I'm not gonna trick you."

No pitcher in his right mind tells the batter what he's going to throw next. And if the batter is Josh Gibson and the bases are loaded, it's just insane! I was sure that Satch was going to fake Josh out and throw a changeup.

But he didn't. He threw an even faster fastball, and he threw it belt high, just like he said he would. Josh swung at it and tipped it back to the catcher's glove. Strike two. The crowd roared again.

"Now I got you 0 and 2, Josh," Satch hollered. You probably think I'm gonna knock you down now. But I ain't gonna throw smoke at your yolk. I'm gonna throw a pea at your knee. Get ready, now."

Flip pulled out the gun again, but it still wouldn't turn on. Why didn't the stupid gun work?! If Satch was *ever* going to throw his hardest pitch, this was the time to do it.

Josh got ready. Satch wound up. He let it fly. Josh swung.

"Strike three!" called the ump. "Yer out!"

"How's that, big man?" Satch yelled as the crowd went crazy. "There ain't a man alive who hits my fast one! There ain't a man alive who shuts my mouth! And you owe me five bucks!"

The game was over. Josh threw his bat all the way into the outfield and stormed to the dugout.

Flip and I made our way toward the exit and out

to the gate near Boquet Street, where Satch had told us to meet him. We knew it would be a while, so we waited patiently. We were still standing there after most of the crowd had left the ballpark.

Flip was still bummed out because the radar gun had gone on the fritz at the exact moment we needed it. While we waited at the corner, I asked him if I could look at the gun.

I opened the battery compartment and took out the batteries. They looked okay. Maybe there was some dirt in there. My dad once told me that if you wet both ends of a battery and clean off the two contacts, that will sometimes make it work. I did that, and then put the batteries back into the gun. When I pushed the Power button, the light flashed on.

Flip slapped his forehead. If only we had done that earlier! Satch probably threw a 100-mile-an-hour fastball to Josh. Maybe 105!

A bus was coming down the street, and Flip pointed the gun at it. He pushed the button, and the screen flashed "42." The gun worked perfectly.

The bus pulled up in front of us and a bunch of people got off. We didn't pay much attention to them. We were talking about how frustrated we were that we hadn't clocked Satch's fastballs to Josh. That's what we were doing when somebody tapped Flip on the shoulder.

"Remember me?"

We turned around.

It was Laverne.

17

A Great Idea

I COULDN'T BELIEVE IT. LAVERNE MUST HAVE TAKEN buses all the way from South Carolina. She had her suitcase with her.

"I'm eighteen years old now," she said. "My father can't tell me what to do anymore."

I wished her a happy birthday, but Laverne wasn't paying much attention to me. She wrapped her arms around Flip, and it didn't look like she was ever going to let go. While they were hugging, I could see the look on Flip's face. I had never seen him so happy.

That's when a great idea popped into my head. It was such a simple and brilliant idea, I don't know why I hadn't thought of it earlier.

I could go back home and leave Flip in 1942.

The wheels were turning in my head now. It would be so easy. I could go duck into a bathroom or something, take out one of my new baseball cards, and send myself back to my own time. *Alone*. I'd leave Flip here. He's eighteen years old. He's young. He's strong. He's got a girl who obviously loves him, and he seems to love her. He could live his whole adult life over again. It would be perfect.

Almost as soon as I thought of this great idea, I started to think that maybe it wasn't so perfect after all. In fact, maybe it was the dumbest idea in history. First of all, who am I to mess with someone else's life? If anyone should make a decision like that, it should be Flip. But I knew that if I mentioned it to him, he would never go for it. He'd say it wasn't "the right thing to do."

Also, if I left Flip in 1942 and he lived his life all over again, who knows what might happen to him? Maybe he would get drafted and have to fight in World War II. Maybe he'd get injured or even killed. Or maybe he would never move to Louisville. Either way, I would get back home and there would *be* no Flip. I'd never have the chance to know him. And it would be my own fault.

There I go again, only thinking of myself. But as I saw the look on his face as he was hugging Laverne, all I could think of was how sad and lonely he was as an old man in the twenty-first century. Any other life must be better.

I was so confused. It was one of those times when you just don't know which *is* the right thing to do.

It was starting to get dark out. There was only

one other car in the parking lot besides Satch's car. Finally, Satch walked out the front entrance.

"Man, I was tossin' them in good," he said to me. "Did you get me on that speed gun of yours? How fast was I?"

"It didn't work," I said, and his face fell. "But I fixed it."

"Come on, let's go back in the ballpark," Satch said. "My arm is still loose. I wanna see what it can do."

"Sure, if you can pull those two apart," I said.

Flip and Laverne were all lovey-dovey, kissing and telling each other how wonderful the other one was. It was starting to get a little gross.

"That girl ain't never gonna let him go," Satch said, shaking his head. "You can't convince a woman about hardly anything. Once they put their minds on it, that's where their minds stay. We might have to turn the hoses on 'em."

But finally, Flip and Laverne managed to pull their lips apart. I told them we were going to go back inside Forbes Field and see how fast Satch could throw a ball. At first Laverne didn't believe it was possible to do such a thing, but we showed her the radar gun and just told her it was a "new invention."

Forbes Field was all locked up by that time, but Satch found a security guy and slipped him a dollar to let us inside the front gate.

"Turn the lights on, will ya, Herbie?" Satch asked him. "It's dark as pitch out."

The lights flashed on. I had never been inside an empty ballpark at night before. It was beautiful. So quiet and peaceful. It was a little eerie too.

"How did you strike out Josh?" I asked Satch as we made our way toward the field.

"Simple," he replied. "I know his weakness."

"Josh has a weakness?" Flip asked.

"Every man has a weakness," Satch said. "With Josh, you tell him exactly what you're gonna throw, and then you throw it. He don't know whether to believe you or not, and it drives him crazy. You gotta work his head. Psychologize him."

We got down to the field and Satch rounded up some catcher's gear and a few baseballs from a closet in the back of the dugout.

"Hey, can we see how fast Flip can throw the ball?" Laverne asked.

"Sure thing," Satch said.

I knew Satch was anxious to throw himself, but he was also a perfect gentleman around ladies. He strapped on the chest protector and put the catcher's mask over his head. Then he handed Flip a baseball. Flip gave me the radar gun and I decided to be a gentleman too.

"Would you like to do the honors?" I asked Laverne.

"Sure!" she said, taking the gun.

I took her about ten yards behind home plate and showed her which button to push. Then I went out to the mound, where Satch and Flip were talking.

"Any words of advice, Satch?" Flip asked.

"Yeah," Satch said quietly, "you got a second chance. That don't happen every day. You better not let that girl get away this time."

"No, I mean *pitching* advice."

"Throw *hard*," Satch said, and he went to squat behind the plate.

I stood off to the side a little. Flip smoothed the dirt in front of the pitching rubber, and then he tossed in a few pitches nice and easy.

"62 miles an hour," Laverne called out. "68 miles an hour. Is that fast?"

"Not bad for a boy," Satch said.

Flip turned it up a notch, throwing a couple of pitches in the mid-70s.

"Okay, give it a little gas now," Satch hollered.

Flip went into his windup, throwing one pitch at 84 miles an hour and the next at 87.

"Is that as hard as you can throw it?" I asked.

"Just about," Flip replied.

"Gimme some smoke," Satch said. "Gimme all you got."

Flip nodded, and threw the ball so hard he nearly toppled off the mound.

"93 miles an hour!" shouted Laverne. "Ya-hoooo!!"

"And he's still a growin' boy," Satch said. "Gettin' stronger every day. I couldn't throw nearly that hard when I was your age."

"Hey," Flip said, "remember that Hesitation Pitch

you told us about? Can you teach me how to throw that?"

Satch walked out to the mound.

"A guy named Plunk Drake taught me the Hesitation back in 1930," he said. "When you're windin' up, you gotta pause a second with your arms up in the air. Then you throw your foot forward, but don't come around with your arm right away. You put the foot down, and then release the ball. Your arm moves slow but the ball moves fast. Throws batters way off stride. Here, lemme show you."

It looked like the perfect opportunity for me. The three of them would be occupied for a while. I decided to make my move.

"I gotta pee," I said.

I ran to the dugout. There were a few doors in the back. I pulled them all open until I found the bathroom.

Quickly, I sat down and pulled out my new baseball cards. I stuffed them all back in my pocket except for one. I didn't even bother looking to see who was on the card. Any new card would get me home.

I closed my eyes.

Sometimes it's hard to know what the right thing to do is. Maybe it was crazy to go back home and leave Flip in 1942 to live his life over again. Maybe it wasn't. Flip always said you should do the right thing. I felt like this was the right thing to do.

There was only one way to find out. Sometimes you just have to take a chance and hope you made the smart decision.

I pinched the card between two fingers and thought about going home. Louisville. The twenty-first century. Soon, I started to feel the slightest tingling sensation in my fingertips. I knew that in a few seconds, I would be going back.

And that's when the bathroom door opened.

18

The Moment of Truth

"WHAT ARE YOU DOING, STOSH?" FLIP ASKED.

I dropped the card. There was nothing I could say. He caught me red-handed.

"I . . . uh . . ."

"You were going to go home without me!" Flip said, his voice rising in anger.

"But, Flip," I said desperately, "it would be perfect! If you stay here, you'll have Laverne. You can live your life all over again. Maybe you can even try out for the Dodgers this time. It would be for the best, Flip! You always said youth is wasted on the young. You wished you knew back when you were young what you know now. Remember? You said you would do things differently. You can take all that knowledge you accumulated in 72 years and start over as an 18-year-old. That would be so cool! I really think you should stay here, Flip."

Flip sighed.

"Stosh, ever since we got here and I saw I was young, I've been thinkin' the same thing," he said. "I've been thinkin' of tellin' you I might stay here."

"So *do* it!" I said.

"I can't," Flip said. "I got the store to take care of, and the team."

"The team?!" I couldn't believe he was worried about my team. "It's just a Little League team, Flip! It's not important. You'll have a new *life* here. A better life."

"I've lived my life, Stosh," he said. "I don't want to live it all over again. Once is enough."

I wasn't going to talk him into staying. He was set in his ways. That's one thing about old people. They can be so stubborn. So I thought of the next best thing.

"Then let's take Laverne back home *with* us, Flip!" I said. "If I can take one person with me, I can probably take two."

"I thought of that," Flip said. "But she's 18 years old, Stosh. When we get back home, I'm gonna be 72 again. She's not gonna want me in our time. And she wouldn't go with us anyway. If we told her we're from the future, she'd think we were crazy. You're a great friend, Stosh. I really appreciate you tryin' to help me. But it just wouldn't work."

"Hey!" Satch yelled from the field. "Will you two hurry it up? My arm's gettin' stiff from lack of grease."

Flip and I went back out to the field. Satch had taken off the chest protector and the catcher's mask. Laverne helped Flip put them on. He crouched behind the plate and Satch went out to the mound.

"Be ready now," Satch said, "'cause I'm throwin' hard."

He buzzed the first pitch in, and it slapped into the mitt with a loud pop.

"90 miles per hour," Laverne called out.

"Now watch this," Satch said.

He threw again, and the gun clocked the pitch at 91. The next two pitches were 92 and 93.

Laverne said the gun was getting a little bit too heavy for her to hold. I took it from her and she moved off to the side.

"Can you throw that fast consistently?" Flip asked.

"Nope, I do it all the time," Satch replied. Then he threw the next pitch 94 miles per hour, and the one after that was 95.

"Ya-hoooo!" shouted Laverne, "If you were white, you would be in the majors for sure."

"Yeah," Satch said, "*if.*"

She meant well, but Laverne's comment seemed to take something out of Satch. I could see his shoulders sag and his head hang a little. I guess he had forgotten about his situation for the moment. Laverne had reminded him that he was the best pitcher in baseball but he was banned from playing at the highest level because of the color of his skin.

"Maybe I should hang 'em up," Satch said. "Only guy I can't strike out is Jim Crow. You don't keep swingin' when a fight's all over."

Flip pulled off the catcher's mask and ran out to the mound.

"Satch, quitting would be a *big* mistake," he said seriously. "You gave me a lotta advice. Now lemme give you some. You're gonna make the majors. You're gonna be very famous one day. You'll be in the Hall of Fame. You gotta believe me. You can't give up now."

"No kiddin'?" Satch said softly. "Hall of Fame?"

"I shouldn't have told you," Flip said. "But it's the truth."

"Then get back behind the plate," Satch said, more confidence in his voice. "Let's see how speedy I can wing this thing."

Flip put the catcher's mask back on and took his position. I aimed the gun. Satch wound up again and burned one in.

"97 miles an hour," I hollered.

The next one clocked at 98, and the one after that was 99 miles per hour. I'm sure Flip's hand was killing him, but he wasn't complaining.

"Okay," Satch said, "I'm gonna cut one loose now. Be ready."

Satch went into his windup. He kicked that leg way up high. He brought that slingshot of an arm down and let it fly. It was the moment of truth.

The instant the ball slammed into the mitt,

there was a *crack*. It sounded like a gunshot.

In fact, it *was* a gunshot. Suddenly, the radar gun just *exploded* in my hand. I mean, it disintegrated. Pieces of plastic went flying everywhere. I closed my eyes so they wouldn't blind me. When I opened them again, the gun was gone. All that was left in my hand was the handle.

"Laverne!" a voice shouted from across the ballpark. "Get over here!"

"It's my father!" Laverne shrieked.

"Uh-oh," Satch said as he ran off the mound. "We better do some fast steppin'. He sounds mighty perturbed."

What happened next was a blur. The four of us went running in different directions. I heard Laverne screaming and her father yelling at her. There was another gunshot.

The lights in Forbes Field suddenly went out. I couldn't see three feet in front of me. I tripped over something and fell down in the dark. I was afraid to make a noise.

"Where are you, boy?" Laverne's father shouted. He was somewhere in the infield now, walking around. "When I find you, I'm gonna kill you."

I didn't know if the "boy" he was talking about was me or Flip or Satch. I wasn't going to take any chances. I crawled down into the dugout on the first base side and took a baseball card out of my pocket. In the distance, I heard an engine start and a car peel away. It was probably Satch, making a getaway.

"Where are you, Laverne?" her father said. "I ain't gonna hurt you, sweetheart. I just want *him*."

Wherever Laverne was hiding, she didn't answer. Her father's voice was closer to me now. He was right outside the dugout. A few feet away. If he came into the dugout, he could trip right over me. Then I'd *really* be in trouble. I wondered where Flip and Laverne were. I hoped they were together.

I could hear my heart pounding in my chest. His footsteps were on the dirt right outside the dugout now. I held the baseball card in my hand and tried to keep my breathing quiet. I had no choice. I had to get out of there. I just wanted to go back to Louisville. I had to leave Flip behind.

Soon the tingling sensation came. It started in my fingertips and moved up my arm. Across my body. Down my legs.

He was in the dugout now. I could hear him breathing. I smelled alcohol. And just before he would have bumped into me, I disappeared.

19

Another Life

I WAS AFRAID TO OPEN MY EYES. I WAS AFRAID OF WHAT I might see. Or what I might *not* see.

What if I arrived back in the twenty-first century and Flip's Fan Club was gone? What if Flip Valentini had died years earlier and he never opened up the store? Or what if he settled down in Atlanta or Los Angeles or someplace other than Louisville? What if I did something or simply *said* something back in 1942 that changed history forever? It would be my fault. Whatever good or bad that had resulted from my actions would be my responsibility.

I opened my eyes.

I was in Flip's Fan Club. I breathed a sigh of relief.

There was good old Flip behind the counter, wrinkled and stooped over. Everything in the store looked just the same.

A little girl and her mother were talking to Flip. I remembered them. They had been asking about Barbie cards the last time I was in the store. The girl wanted to buy new Barbie cards, but Flip only had some old ones to sell.

"Can I have your autograph, Mr. Valentini?" the girl asked. "It's for my cousin's birthday. He's a big fan."

A big fan? Of Flip? That was strange. Why would anyone want Flip's autograph?

"How much do you charge?" the girl's mother asked, opening her purse and taking out her wallet.

This was *too* weird. Somebody was willing to pay Flip for his autograph? I must have been hallucinating.

"Fuhgetaboutit," Flip said. "What's your cousin's name?"

"Steven," the girl said.

Flip reached under the counter and took out a black-and-white photo of a baseball player who looked a lot like Flip. He wrote across the bottom with a black marker:

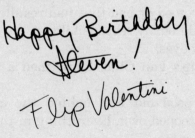

I looked at the photo. It was a guy in a Brooklyn Dodgers uniform. He was winding up to pitch. Now I was *sure* I was hallucinating.

Flip handed the photo to the girl, and she held it like it was a treasure. She and her mom must have thanked Flip about ten times before they finally left the store.

"Stosh!" Flip said after the door jangled shut. "How ya doin'?"

"You . . . you played in the majors?" I croaked.

Flip looked at me strangely.

"You *know* I played in the majors," he said. "Are you okay, Stosh?"

"I think I need some water," I replied.

While Flip went to get me a drink, I looked around the store. At first it looked like everything was the same. But then I looked at the photos of the old Brooklyn Dodgers on the wall. Jackie Robinson, Pee Wee Reese, Duke Snider. I'd seen those photos a hundred times. But there was something different about them now. I went over for a closer look.

There *was* a difference. There was a second person in each photo now. And the second person was Flip! *Young* Flip.

I thought I might faint.

Next to the photos were some yellowed old newspaper clippings, and they were all articles about Flip. I scanned the headlines. FLIP FLIPS CARDINALS IN 3-1 VICTORY . . . VALENTINI WINS 20TH GAME . . . FLIP VALENTINI ANNOUNCES RETIREMENT.

The last one was dated 1963. I read the first paragraph:

> *Flip Valentini, fireballer who pitched*
> *with the Dodgers, Cincinnati Reds,*
> *and Pittsburgh Pirates over a long*
> *and productive National League*
> *career, retired yesterday after his 18th*
> *season. Valentini finished his career*
> *with 287 wins, 2,856 strikeouts, and*
> *an earned run average of 2.87. He had*
> *an overpowering fastball, but credited*
> *his success to his baffling Hesitation*
> *Pitch, which he learned from the great*
> *Satchel Paige before either of them*
> *reached the majors.*

"Are you okay, Stosh?"

I turned around to see an old lady standing there. She handed me a glass of water and held the back of her hand against my forehead, just like my mom does when she thinks I'm coming down with something. Flip was standing behind her.

"Who are you?" I asked, taking a sip.

"See what I mean, Laverne?" Flip said. "We should call his mother."

"*Laverne?*" I asked. "You're Laverne?!"

I searched the old lady's face. Her hair was gray and her skin was wrinkled, but it *was* Laverne! I could see a faint resemblance in her eyes.

"Well, of *course* I'm Laverne, you silly willie," she said, chuckling. "Who else would I be?"

Suddenly it was all clear to me. I had traveled back to 1942 with Flip. We met Satchel Paige, and Satch taught him how to throw the Hesitation Pitch. We also met Laverne in 1942, and she and Flip fell in love. When Laverne's dad went psycho and tried to shoot us, I had to leave Flip behind and come back to the twenty-first century by myself. After I left, Flip and Laverne must have run off together, and Flip must have tried out for the Dodgers. He had a baseball career. He had a new life. And now Flip and Laverne were an old married couple!

"You're just a little dizzy, Stosh," Laverne said. "You'll be fine. Flip, will you please call up Mrs. Stoshack and ask her to come get him?"

Flip was about to pick up the phone, when it rang.

"Hello?" he said into the receiver. "Yeah, this is Flip Valentini. . . . Very funny . . . You're kiddin' me. . . . You sure this ain't some joke? . . . Okay, thanks."

Flip let the phone fall back on the hook. He had sort of a glassy-eyed look on his face.

"What is it?" Laverne asked. "Is something wrong? Did somebody die?"

"You'll never believe me," Flip said.

"Try me," said Laverne.

"Not in a million years," Flip said.

"What happened?" I asked.

"They voted me into the Baseball Hall of Fame."

For a moment, the three of us just stood there. It was like somebody had just told me that an elephant had landed on the moon. It was so different from anything I expected to hear that I didn't know how to react.

But it wasn't long until we were all screaming and jumping up and down and hugging one another. Somebody must have seen us through the window, because people started streaming in to congratulate Flip. Soon the tiny store was jammed with people, and we were in the middle of a party. Somebody produced a bottle of champagne and squirted it at Flip. The phone started ringing and it didn't stop.

After about an hour, Laverne told everybody that all the excitement had tired Flip out and he had to go home and rest. I was about to leave when she pulled me aside.

"None of this would have happened if it wasn't for you," she whispered in my ear. "You realize that, don't you? Flip and I owe everything to you. Will you come join us for dinner tonight?"

"What are you having?" I asked.

"Roast chicken and corn bread," she told me. "It'll make you think you died and went to heaven."

She was right. Dinner was great. Flip and Laverne had a nice house too, much nicer than the dumpy apartment Flip used to live in. He seemed so much happier now.

While we were eating, the conversation turned to baseball, as it usually did whenever Flip was around. Laverne said it would be interesting to travel to the *future* to see what baseball would look like a hundred years from now. But that would be impossible, Flip and I pointed out. I always go to the year on the card. I would need a future card to go to the future, and obviously, future cards don't exist until you get there. Flip suggested some players from the past I might want to visit, like Roberto Clemente, Ty Cobb, or Ted Williams. I tossed out Joe DiMaggio and Hank Greenberg.

It was a great evening, for all of us. The only disappointment, we all agreed, was that we never did clock Satch's best stuff on the radar gun.

"Now that it's all over," I asked Flip, "how fast do you think Satch really was? Do you think he could have thrown 105 miles an hour?"

"Maybe it's none of our business," Flip replied. "Some legends oughta stay legends. Some mysteries oughta stay mysteries. It'd be nice to know, but it's better to wonder."

Facts and Fictions

Everything in this book is true, except for the stuff I made up. It's only fair to tell you which is which.

From 1898 to 1946, African Americans were banned from professional baseball for no other reason than the color of their skin. Many of the greatest players in history never played major league baseball.

Satchel Paige was arguably the greatest pitcher who ever lived, and certainly the most quotable. (Much of his dialog in this book was spoken or written by Satch himself.) Negro League statistics were not always written down, but Satch claimed to have pitched 2,600 games and won 2,100 of them. He also said he pitched 300 shutouts and 55 no-hitters. Of course, Satch was known to have stretched the truth on occasion.

Satch really did drive his car (and sometimes fly his own plane) to games, rather than take the team bus. He pitched for any team that would pay him, sometimes blowing into town and fronting a hastily assembled team of local amateurs (like the New York Stars) for one game. The Indianapolis Clowns, however, were a real Negro League team. A young Hank Aaron, by the way, started out on the Clowns at age eighteen.

Satch really did call in his fielders sometimes and strike out the side, and he really was served with divorce papers by somebody pretending to want an autograph.

I played a little fast and loose with the facts about the 1942 Negro League World Series. It was actually Game Two when Satch walked two batters intentionally so he could pitch to Josh Gibson with the bases loaded. That incident took place in the seventh inning, not the ninth. Satch pitched in all four of the World Series games that year, and he won three of them.

After a long Negro League career, Satch finally made his first major league appearance for the Cleveland Indians on July 9, 1948. He was 42 years old by then, and possibly older. (Satch was always cagey about his age.) Satch won six games and lost just one that year, helping the Indians win the American League pennant. (The league banned the Hesitation Pitch as soon as Satch used it.)

But he still wasn't finished. Satch went on to pitch four more seasons. Finally, after being out of the big leagues for a dozen years, the Kansas City Athletics brought him back for one last appearance on September 25, 1965. Satch was almost sixty years old. He pitched three shutout innings that day. It had been nearly forty years from his first professional game until his last.

In 1971, Satchel Paige became the first Negro League player inducted into the Baseball Hall of Fame. He died on June 8, 1982, in Kansas City. He is buried there, in Forest Hill Memorial Park Cemetery.

Just as Satchel Paige was quite possibly the best pitcher ever, Josh Gibson may have been the game's greatest hitter. He hit around 800 home runs in his career, with a batting average of .352. In exhibition games against major league pitchers, he hit an incredible .426.

But by 1942, Josh had begun to fade. He was experiencing bouts of dizziness and headaches. He only made 2 hits in 13 at bats in that 1942 World Series.

Four months later, on New Year's Day, 1943, Josh fainted and was in a coma for ten days. It was determined that he had a brain tumor. Josh refused to have an operation to remove it, and things got worse. Over the next four years, Josh suffered from nervous breakdowns, hallucinations, alcoholism, and addiction to heroin. After several suicide attempts, he was briefly admitted to a mental hospital.

On Sunday, January 19, 1947, Josh went to a movie. When the lights came up, he was found slumped in his seat. He died in the middle of the night at his mother's house. He was only 35 years old.

Nobody knows if Josh died from a brain hemorrhage, a stroke, or a drug overdose. Some say he died of a broken heart. He had hit more home runs than Babe Ruth, but he never was allowed to play in the big leagues. He was virtually unknown outside the world of black baseball.

Josh Gibson was buried in an unmarked grave in Pittsburgh's Allegheny Cemetery. Twenty-five years later, his accomplishments were recognized and he became the second Negro League player inducted into the Baseball Hall of Fame. Money was raised for a proper gravestone.

Ten weeks after Josh died, Jackie Robinson (who played with Satch on the Kansas City Monarchs in 1945) broke the color barrier. White baseball began snatching up the best Negro League players, such as Hank Aaron and Willie Mays. Fans stopped going to Negro League games and the league went out of business. The last Negro League World Series was played in 1948.

Stosh, Laverne, and Flip Valentini do not exist in the real world (though I do have an old friend named Fred Valentini).

And you can't travel through time. At least not yet.

Read More!

Most of the information in this book came from reading lots of books about Satchel Paige, Josh Gibson, and the Negro Leagues. If you'd like to learn more, ask your librarian for these:

Bruce, Janet. *The Kansas City Monarchs: Champions of Black Baseball*. Lawrence, Kans.: University Press of Kansas, 1985.

Eckstut, Arielle, and David Sterry, editors. *Satchel Sez: The Wit, Wisdom, and World of Leroy "Satchel" Paige*. New York: Three Rivers Press, 2001.

Heward, Bill, with Dimitri V. Gat. *Some Are Called Clowns: A Season with the Last of the Great Barnstorming Baseball Teams*. New York: Crowell, 1974.

Holway, John. *Blackball Stars: Negro League Pioneers*. Westport, Conn.: Meckler, 1988.

Holway, John. *Josh and Satch: The Life and Times of Josh Gibson and Satchel Paige*. New York: Carroll & Graf, 1992.

Paige, Leroy Satchel, as told to David Lipman. *Maybe I'll Pitch Forever*. New York: Doubleday, 1962.

Paige, Leroy Satchel, as told to Hal Lebovitz. *Pitchin' Man: Satchel Paige's Own Story*. Westport, Conn.: Meckler, 1948.

Peterson, Robert. *Only the Ball Was White*. Englewood Cliffs, N.J.: Prentice-Hall, 1970.

Ribowsky, Mark. *Don't Look Back: Satchel Paige in the Shadows of Baseball*. New York: Simon & Schuster, 1994.

Ribowsky, Mark. *The Power and the Darkness: The Life of Josh Gibson in the Shadows of the Game*. New York: Simon & Schuster, 1996.

Rogosin, Donn. *Invisible Men: Life in Baseball's Negro Leagues*. New York: Macmillan, 1985.

Satchel Paige's Rules for Staying Young

—Avoid fried meats which angry up the blood.

—If your stomach disputes you, lie down and pacify it with cool thoughts.

—Keep the juices flowing by jangling around gently as you move.

—Go very light on the vices, such as carrying on in society—the social ramble ain't restful.

—Avoid running at all times.

—And don't look back. Something might be gaining on you.

Permissions

The author would like to acknowledge the following for use of photographs and artwork: National Baseball Hall of Fame Library, Cooperstown, NY: 26, 36, 59, 104, 110. George Strock/Time Life Pictures/Getty Images: 72. Nina Wallace: 7, 99, 132. Collection of John Holway: 134, 144.

"Satchel Paige's Rules for Staying Young" were originally published in *Collier's* magazine, June 13, 1953.

About the Author

Satch & Me is Dan Gutman's seventh Baseball Card Adventure. He is also the author of *The Kid Who Ran for President, The Million Dollar Shot, Johnny Hangtime, The Get Rich Quick Club*, the My Weird School series, and many other books for young people. Dan lives in New Jersey with his wife, Nina, and their two children. If you would like to find out more about Dan or his books, visit his website: www.dangutman.com.